VICE AVENGED
A Moral Tale

VICE AVENGED

A Moral Tale

◞◟

LOLAH BURFORD

THE MACMILLAN COMPANY
NEW YORK, NEW YORK

The Macmillan Company
866 Third Avenue, New York, N.Y. 10022
Collier-Macmillan Canada Ltd., Toronto, Ontario

Library of Congress Catalog Card Number: 78–136261

First Printing

Printed in the United States of America

To GEORGETTE HEYER

CONTENTS

AUTHOR'S NOTE

Here is an eighteenth-century fairy tale, frankly unserious, frankly unrealistic, for a realistic, serious Age. I will not call it fantastic, our age is far more fantastic, but let us remember that *serious* was a derogative word then, and *realistic* was still only a technical term of the philosophers. Why is it a fairy tale? Because it is an unlikely combination of the novel of manners with the novel of sex, and in it uninvolvement becomes involvement, the inhuman human, and power becomes powerless. Like all fairy tales, it exists for its own sake and in its own world, asking only "that willing suspension of disbelief for the moment that constitutes poetic faith." It is an adolescent daydream with echoes of reality, suggesting the lines of Pope so popular with the male literary world of the eighteenth century: "Ev'ry woman is at heart a rake." It is also, of course, beyond its absurdities a spiritual allegory: *Caveat lector.*

Should one apologize for another piece of late eighteenth-century nonsense? Of escapist froth blowing off a small deal of fact? I think not: I have noticed that eighteenth-century and early nineteenth-century novels go first and most constantly off the library shelves. The private coach still exercises its hold, above the public airplane and the demanding machine, and in it Lady Caroline still says to Lord Byron:

9

When first you told me in the Carriage to kiss your mouth & I durst
not—& after thinking it such a crime it was more than I could prevent from that moment—was I cold then—were you so?—When my
heart did not meet yours but flew before it—

The small deal of fact has to do with the notorious Hell-
Fire clubs and their count of rakehells that flourished throughout the eighteenth century under various names, among them
the early Mohocks and the later Monks of Medmenham
Abbey. They struck my imagination years ago when I was
reading in a course in eighteenth-century literature. The
unbelieving reader may find muted descriptions of these
societies of noble young (and not so young) rakes in *The
Clubs of Augustan London*, Robert J. Allen, Archon Books,
1967, as well as in the general literature and correspondence
of the period. Let these two contemporary letters give a brief
idea of a milder part of their nature. Thomas Burnett (himself
reputed a Mohock) writes this way:

There have of late been about the Town a sett of young fellows that
called themselves Mohocks . . . These men used to . . . beat Watch-
men, slit fellows noses and cut women's arms, stop coaches or chairs,
and offer violence to Ladys even of Quality.

The Schemers are described by Lady Mary Wortley Montague:

Twenty very pretty fellows (the Duke of Wharton being president
and chief director) have formed themselves into a committee of gallantry. They call themselves *Schemers*; and meet regularly three times
a week, to consult on gallant schemes for the advantage and advance-
ment of that branch of happiness . . .

The rest of the passage has been excised by Lady Mary's early editor as too indelicate for ears other than her correspondent's. Such societies and such Hell-Fire clubs are rumored to exist throughout the eighteenth century. The betting book at White's (first a chocolate-coffee-gaming house, later a club) may still be read through, although several of the bets have been scratched out by later censors. A "hell" was simply a gambling house, usually with the front of being a supper club.

Meanwhile, go, little book, and show Virtue her image through Vice.

Plus ne suis ce que j'ai été
Et plus ne saurais jamais l'être.
Mon beau printemps et mon été
Ont fait le saut par la fenêtre.
Amour, tu as été mon maître,
Je t'ai servi sur tous les dieux.
Ah, si je pouvais deux fois naître,
Combien je te servirais mieux.

I am no more what I have been
And I can never more be it.
My lovely spring and my summer
Have made the leap out of the window.
Love, thou hast been my master,
I have served thee over all the gods.
Ah, if I could be twice born,
How much better I should serve thee.

French song, seventeenth century

VICE AVENGED
A Moral Tale

I

THE GAME

They were sitting in a hell, one night, the Marquis and his special friends. They were tired of cards, the hour was close to four, and they had tried a touch of the new weed that certain of the more unconventional bucks were using, in place of snuff. They cast about for further amusement, idly. They sat like beautiful birds, in their bright shining colours, their hair elaborately dressed, their long graceful fingers lying careless on the table among the equipment of the game, seeming frail, their hard and very real power masked under the lace. In reality, they were a kind of bird of prey, the lines of the downcast nose severe and beaked, the glint in the eye hooded under an effect of ease.

"Lord, I'm bored," said the youngest, Viscount Teviot, "I've only lost four thousand, and where's the fun in it?"

"Les jeux dangereux, mon vieux, that's what you need," the Honourable Frederic said, lazily turning his head.

"Holding up stages on Hounslow Heath?" enquired the Marquis of Gore rudely. "That's not for me."

"In London Street, Gore," corrected the Honourable Frederic pedantically. "With your name, I'd think you would."

"You insult my name?" said the Marquis silkily as his coat, not looking up.

"Lord, I don't, I don't! But what a bloody title. Demned suggestive, and well put."

"It don't mean what you think. It's from a spot some ancestor of mine claimed, but we can't find."

"You don't need the rent?" asked the Viscount Teviot.

"I don't. *Jeux dangereux,*" he repeated. "What do you have in mind?"

They sat in silence, considering.

"I am bored with respectability," proffered the Viscount Lisle, yawning. *"Faisons le scandale, je pense."*

The Marquis' eyebrows lifted.

"It's the only thing that isn't done," the Viscount Lisle explained, with an amused gleam. "I mean, all this," he waved a hand to include the cards and gaming things, "and even this," indicating the weed, "and Hounslow Heath, and Gore's petite Birds of Paradise—the pikesticks may frown on, but no one else does. I mean, so many of us do it, it is really quite the thing. And easy to make safe. It's lost the thrill for me, I mean, it's getting stiff. Now what I'd like to do is something there's some risk to, something—"

"Epouvantable?" suggested the Viscount Rockfort.

"Something the ladies in their salons wouldn't care to whisper over," the Viscount Lisle finished with a certain sudden viciousness, "—of a sort our less regrettable, less daring friends would not pass over if they knew, but which they would not know."

"Then where's the thrill in it?" asked the Honourable Freddie.

"I think he means the doing should suffice," the Viscount Rockfort leaned over to say, looking interested.

"I can't imagine what you have in mind," said the Marquis. "But I sense you do have something on it. Spit it out."

"I suggest that we seduce the quality," said the Viscount Lisle, leisurely watching the effect of his suggestion.

"Good God, not Lady Jersey!" said the Marquis. "I protest. That goes too far. Boredom much to be preferred. Anyhow, it's been done before."

"Lord, Bysshe, be serious," instructed the Viscount Teviot. The Marquis again laughed rudely.

"It's done all the time, dear Lisle, you know it well," Rockfort said. "Why do you say it's new?"

"I didn't mean the married quality." Three out of four pairs of eyes now rested on him. "I was thinking of a somewhat rarer diamond, hedged in by some extraordinary circumstance," he continued, changing his metaphor, "tempting in view, but too high on the bough, not plucked and needing it." He smiled. "It might be called a kind of service, even. Think of it: a disastrous season, a sudden death, a blighted tendre, too high an expectation, an absent-minded guardian, a widowed parent neglectful of responsibility, a second sister coming on, brothers whose gaming debts or educations take her dowry—the result, a nubile virgin shelved." His companions showed by their faces they recognised certain stories current in the ton. "I put it we correct the situation."

"If I take your meaning," said the Viscount Rockfort imperturbably, "we are going to make a list of names of chits one might think—impregnable—"

"Is there such thing?" murmured the Honourable Frederic.

"And then we raid the citadel, *c'est tout*," said the Viscount Lisle mischievously.

"Well, who's to know the thing's been really done?" asked Teviot. "I mean, I'd never take the word of Freddie here."

"Say it again," commanded the gentleman in question, but Teviot did not.

"Nature has a way of doing that, my love," the Viscount Lisle replied to Teviot.

"I think you're serious," the Marquis said abruptly. "We must be drunker than I thought."

"Am I ever not serious?" The Viscount Lisle looked about him ironically with wicked eyes. "What do you say?"

"I propose these stakes," offered the Viscount Rockfort without hesitation, matching his look: "a sudden wedding, 5000 lou; a continental trip, 2000 more; convent, double both; a babe within the year, that winner takes all."

The pall of boredom had left the company, and they sent for more wine.

"It sounds promising," said the Marquis quietly. "How do we go about it? This—impregnation—club?"

"I'd say," the Honourable Frederic suggested, "the best would be if there's no stir at all."

"Seduce the chit, you mean?"

"More skill involved, you know," the Honourable Frederic explained.

"What's your proof, and how much time allowed?" pursued the Marquis.

"Gore will bet on anything, he rises to the lure," the Honourable Frederic commented, in an audible aside.

"Oh, something unmistakable. Rockfort can judge."

"Like the gel herself?" the Marquis said with some contempt.

The Viscount Lisle shook his head, choosing to smile. "Too hard. But something irrefutable? And let us place personal bets upon the time." The Viscount again surveyed his audience. "We are then agreed?"

They nodded, half amused, half shocked at themselves. The Viscount applied himself to his work, and after some thought, produced five names which he put in a box. "Shall we game to see who takes the first?"

"Docs the winner go or stay?" the Marquis asked.

"Go, by all means, dear Bysshe. The losers stay."

"Then I might cheat to lose. I'm not sure this is my kind of game," the Marquis suggested.

"I thought it was your field?" the Viscount countered maliciously, with a faint hint of a leer.

"Not quite like this," he murmured. "You flatter me."

"Do you withdraw then?" The Viscount's voice held a more audible gibe.

"No, I'll stay. Deal out."

The next round of cards was played intensely.

Characteristically, the Marquis won. "Oh, lord!" he exclaimed, half in dismay. "I thought I should have stayed away tonight."

"If you cannot do it—?" suggested the Viscount Lisle politely.

"Cannot I? We will see who cannot," the Marquis answered curtly. "Hand me your damned box."

The Marquis drew and unfolded his paper, with a teased smile, while his friends watched with more than usual interest.

"Good lord, I know my chit," said the Marquis frowningly, surveying the little slip he had drawn, and the name of the girl written on it.

The Viscount Lisle paused beside him, attentive—before proffering his little box with its names further.

"Do we not all know them all?" murmured the Viscount Lisle. "Of necessity, being all of the ton?"

"I mean, I really do," the Marquis said, still with a little frown. "I mean I used to. I don't think she knows me."

"You want another name?"

"No. It will do as well as any. It just must be thought out well."

"To Gore and his lady!" The Honourable Frederic lifted his glass and drained it. He was joined by the several Viscounts but not the object of his toast.

The Marquis spoke consideringly: "I think the lady's name should not be told." He looked around him questioningly.

Rockfort nodded his head in agreement. "The Viscount will know the names he has put in, but not who drew each one. Let him judge the proofs—if they are good, he'll know which name."

The Marquis signified his agreement to this speech. He folded his paper carefully into a squib and burned it in a candle flame. He waited patiently until all the little ashes tumbled down, and then he turned, his eyes enigmatic, and said: "There! It is gone. What do you say?" The very chandeliers seemed to wink.

"I say we shall make *le scandale* indeed," said the Honourable Frederic. "I never would have thought of such a sport."

"*Jeux dangereux* indeed," repeated the Marquis thoughtfully, his eyes still on the little heap of ashes. But if he did not approve, he had not said so, nor any of the others. They were not particularly imaginative men. The Marquis, however, was a man of despatch. "I will do it tomorrow night and meet you here again by five, or shortly after." His eyes glinted suddenly and a wicked smile touched his lips. "What stakes I don't?"

The Honourable Frederic laughed, and named his figure.

"Viscount?" The Marquis in turn collected promises from each. He laid his hand on Frederic's shoulder, "Whose turn, I venture, will be next," he said, unpleasantly polite. As the Honourable Frederic laughed uneasily at being so tapped and his friends smiled broadly, the Marquis, his face serene, bowed and went out.

II

THE PREPARING

The Marquis did not go home, to his town house, to sleep. Instead, he roused his valet, nodding in a chair, to lay out the suit he directed, and without changing took his curricle and drove down to his father's estate where he appeared without warning for breakfast. His mother and father were not home; they had left for church already. He restored himself leisurely on ham and ale, looking about him with sleepy interest. The early sunlight filtered through the windows, and fell upon the quiet room and polished furnishings. But if it was a benediction, he thought, it was not for him. He had already ridden up into the hilly woods, before announcing himself at the house, to a hollow a few miles from the house itself which he knew well from his excursions as a boy, and there he had left a pile of carriage robes he had brought down with him from town.

That his father and his mother would not approve of their land being used as he intended did not disturb him in the least. Accustomed to doing exactly as he pleased, he gave that aspect of his adventure little thought. He had come precisely because his father's seat was by cross-country not ten miles from Rotherby, the Duke of Salisbury's country home, and it was there he had his appointment for that night. The Duke of Salisbury was well-known for his hunts, and he understood that the entire family was there in residence for the May Day Hunt.

He rose, suppressing a yawn. He would have liked to go to sleep, but instead he went back to his curricle, which he had not had taken around to the stables, and drove himself into the village to the square squat ivy-covered church where he expected to find his parents. The service had begun, but he strolled in unconcernedly, ignoring the shocked looks directed on him and in his turn staring about him with quizzing glances, his boots clapping lightly against the stone floor, and made his way down to the front pew of his family. He opened the door without hurry, and took his place, not often filled, beside his mother. His father kept his face, rigid with disapproval, turned towards the altar. His mother sent him a look of delighted, delicate surprise, and pressed his hand with her gloved fingers; but sitting directly under the Vicar's expressive disapproving nose, she did not speak. For the remainder of the lesson and the sermon, the Marquis composed himself to sit a model of behaviour except that his eyes were shut and his face looked vacantly bored.

Afterwards, aware his late arrival in bright evening dress and in any case, his presence there at all, had made him a cynosure for all the congregated eyes, he performed his due, standing up with his parents and conversing civilly with their neighbours. He felt no constraint. The Duke of Salisbury and his family patronised a different church more neighbouring to their seat, for by the straight road the distances were long. It was May Day itself, and flowered poles stood about the village green, at a suitable distance from the church, waiting for the afternoon, but the Marquis had no eye for country frolics, this day or any day.

The congregation had dispersed, and the Marquis stood by his curricle. "Bysshe, what a charming surprise to see you!" his mother exclaimed, free now to speak.

"Particularly," added his Grace, "since we have not seen you these six months past, since Christmas."

"I have been occupied, Maman," he said, dutifully kissing her.

"May one ask how?" his father enquired, with faint aversion in his voice.

The Marquis looked back at his father with a similar feeling expressed on his countenance and said lazily, his tone bordering on disrespect: "I work to avert the boredom, and that exhausts me so, I have time for nothing else." He mounted onto the perch of his curricle. "I have come for lunch," he announced largely, inviting himself. "I shall meet you at the house," and whipped his horses, leaving his parents to make whatever remarks they chose without his presence to inhibit them.

His Grace, the Duke of Adversane, lived in comparative retirement. He was a gentle, scholarly, and remote younger son who had had no thoughts of succeeding to the title, and had at one time considered going into the Clergy without distaste. He now overlooked his estates, with his agent, continuing to live where and as he always had, spending his time on his land, grown vaster, or in his library. He had withdrawn some time ago from the social life of the ton, which had never interested him, and he did not hunt. His only son so far seemed to resemble neither himself nor his wife, and was a source of irritation to him, when they infrequently met. The Marquis seemed to be a throwback to her Grace's father, in whom the fiery Irish and the volatile French had improbably mixed. That gentleman, familiarly known as Black Harry, had briefly made his name as one of London's infamous Mohocks before he settled into a comparative respectability. The Duchess, a madcap like her father in her schoolroom days but tamer now in her middle age, managed her house, visited her country neighbours, loved her flamboyant son without knowing much about him, and attempted ineffectually to bridge the widening gap between her husband and her son. The two had few points in common beyond the fact of siring. The Marquis in his view of books was closer to his paternal grandfather who had once shouted at an enquiring child, later the Marquis' father: "These books of mine are for my library, they are not to read!" The Marquis could read, but once released from school, he did not choose to. Ripples of his London life occasionally broke the calm of his parents' peaceful country ways, but they chose not to understand, or perhaps did not. What his father had said to him at their last meeting held true: "We deal best apart."

The Marquis listened politely to various pieces of country news during lunch, his mind on other things. In the steady flow of talk one name pierced through to his mind, and his attention pricked up.

"Salisbury had his Hunt yesterday. You might have gone, had you come then," his father was remarking.

"Did he?" said the Marquis, with no evidence of interest. "Hunting doesn't interest me, I find it something of a bore, and devilish hard on my clothes."

"We share one feeling, then," his father remarked humour-lessly. "I did not go myself."

"Didn't you use to hunt with his two sons, Bysshe?" his mother asked.

"I may have done so. I forget," the Marquis answered vaguely. "I haven't seen them now for years. We're not in the same set."

"You saw them at the Duke's rout just last year, Bysshe. Your father was persuaded just that once to take me up to it."

The Marquis yawned, without concealment. "I forget."

"You have no manners, Bysshe," his father said sharply, "and what you used to have you try to lose. I find it unbecoming in you. You will rely upon your charm too far one day."

"I did not know I had it. You flatter me," the Marquis tossed out, with a surface show of pleasantness.

"I assure you I did not intend to," his father said, with none.

The Marquis looked at him, his gaze unfriendly. "I am what I am. This is the way I am, and this is the way I am going to be. Shall I go?" He made to rise from his chair.

"Your Grace, let be!" his still beautiful mother interposed

with some authority. "Oh, Bysshe, sit down, sit down, and don't behave so stiff. You act as if you hadn't been asleep."

"I haven't," her son admitted ruefully, and suppressed a yawn successfully.

"Did you see his daughter Cressida?" his mother continued, speaking to his Grace.

"She rode right with them, with her father and her brothers. I saw her take the hedge. She did it well."

"I think she would be better staying in the house. Her father and her brothers forget sometimes she's not a boy. I've heard—"

"Is she a hoyden?" interrupted the Marquis, interested. "I thought it was the other way."

"I do not know, I have not met her. But she will never marry if her father does not someday start remembering she's a girl."

The Marquis' interest was further aroused. "What of her mother? Doesn't she see to it, or does she hunt, too?"

"She is dead, Bysshe. You knew that."

The Marquis' face was thoughtful. "I may have known, but I've forgotten, then. I knew her. She was kind to me once when I visited them. You remember that? But the Duke was regularly fierce. Lord, we took his horse out once, and he would have whipped us all. But we didn't stay to receive it, and he thought better by the next day, or she made him think so. I am sorry she is dead. I did not know."

"Of course you knew, Bysshe. You'd forgotten."

"Very well, then, I've forgotten. It does not really matter. It makes no difference to me now." He spoke idly. He was remembering back those many years to the Christmas holiday when his parents had gone abroad to the Continent, and he had visited with the Duke of Salisbury's sons who were then at Eton, too. They had used their sister's room to effect their escape from the angry Duke because her French windows opened out onto a little balcony, and a great beech tree stood near it. Down it they had made good their daring exit from a thoroughly aroused rough justice. He smiled slightly at the memory. He wondered if her room was still the same. "Is the girl out?" he asked.

His mother understood him. "An aunt brought her out two seasons before last year's, or was it further back, but nothing came of it."

"I don't remember it," he said.

The talk passed to other subjects than the Salisbury Hunt, and after a time, the Marquis excused himself. The conversation had set a plan in motion in his mind, and he wished to look into it. He could easily climb that tree alone, but he could not see himself descending it with a struggling chit on his shoulder. He rummaged among his old possessions that had been stored away, as he had left them, in an attic, looking for a rope ladder from his long dismantled tree house. He found it finally, and a domino mask he had used at some long forgotten charade, and his old flask. He visited his mother's dressing room privately, looking for her paregoric sleeping draught. He mixed a portion of it with some water in the flask, and stored his finds in his valise. His preparations made, he returned to the drawing room and his mother. His mother was used to his strange whims. When he told her that he had come to see her, just to go to church with her on May Day, but that he was expected at a London rout that night, she believed him and set dinner ahead for him. His father was displeased.

"Gore," said the Duke, "I wish you would not come walking

into my house without warning, and disarrange my dinner hour." His son's face showed no compunction. His Grace surveyed his lounging son and compressed his lips. "Your coat is cut too tight, Bysshe. The new styles do not please me, they make a man unfit for any use. Can you even raise your arms?"

The Marquis obligingly showed he could. "But I will take your advice, my père, and change into my travelling coat. Robertson rather poured me into this." He surveyed himself complacently in the long mirror of the salon. "I think myself that it looks rather well." But he made no move to leave. The unsuitability of his dress, which clearly indicated he had driven straight down from some late affair without changing, served as a reminder to him of the weird night just past. Contrary to his nature, he found his mind slightly brooding over it, as he sat in the drawing room with his mother, alone now with her.

Under the mellow influence of the familiar house, away from London, he thought the scene in the hell truly from Hell, and that they had been a little mad. He felt tired and unusually dispirited and the night's work he had promised himself had no appeal for him. What a stupid joke, he thought, and how like Lisle who he suspected had no love for women, to coldly rape some unsuspecting girl, just to make a good story. He did not see the fun in it, and certainly no thrill. He felt capable to it, but disinterested; his concern lay more for himself than for the girl, to whom he gave little thought. Nevertheless, he did not seriously consider voiding the bet, and he did not consider at all duping the Viscount Lisle whom he knew to be a strange and dangerous man. He had lost heavily that particular month, and he had bought a second curricle to replace one he had smashed, and he still owed for his yacht, and the Devil knew what to his tailor. It was only the gaming debts that he seldom had that he would have to pay, but "I cannot even do that," he thought. It would be useless to apply for extra money to his father. The Duke did not keep him on a tight leash, he had to admit in fairness to him, but the limits of his generosity had been clearly set. Lisle had the money he himself was thought to have, and so had Frederic, and he could use it. His mother, he realised, was still talking to him. He bent to catch her words.

"You are not attending me, Gore," she said crossly.

"Indeed I was, Maman."

"You were not. Tell me what I just said."

"You told me"—he paused—"that you and Adversane intend to sell this seat and move to London." His eyes briefly sparked with mischief.

"You see, you were not listening at all. No, I shall not tell you after all again. It concerned your Cousin Anne and your friend Lynton, the younger one. They are engaged."

"Lynton? I don't believe it. I just saw him, and he didn't look like an engaged man. He looked quite happy, and just the same."

"Nevertheless, it is quite true."

"Poor Lynton then and poor Anne," he said lazily, still not really attending.

She looked at him thoughtfully, but she decided against entering into an argument they had discussed many times before. She knew she could not change him. Still she wondered sometimes why he found her pleasant marriage with his father no inducement towards the same estate.

Adversane came in then, a frown on his brow. "The kitchen servants want to put up a Maypole on our green here, but I have told them flatly *no*."

"Why not? I think the dance is pretty," the Duchess asked innocently. "I said they might."

"It is a frank and open invitation to the strongest kind of lechery," his Grace said still frowningly.

His son was overcome. He leaned back against his chair, and laughed hysterically, too loudly and much too long. His mother looked at him perplexed and his father scowled at him angrily. When finally he brought himself under control, he said, between gasps: "You are too scholarly, my sire. They'd never think of it, if you had not told them so. I suppose you did? Oh, lord, I'd have liked to see their faces," and he fell helpless victim to his mirth again.

His Grace only said with dignity: "I have asked you, Bysshe, to not say *lord* in such a way on Sunday in my house. If you cannot refrain, please keep your Sunday routs in London by yourself."

"Your pardon, sire," his son said easily, with no noticeable penitence. He strolled to the window. "I see they have the Maypole up," he said lazily. "It's all fixed up with flowers and little posies; it looks quite harmless there to me. Will you make them pull it down?" His humour threatened to overcome him again, and he felt almost drunk. The look of angry humiliation on his father's face suddenly sobered him, and he said again, this time sincerely: "Your pardon, sire."

"You are incorrigible, I think, Bysshe," his father said with distaste, and walked from the room.

His mother, remaining with him, observed the Marquis'

frequent yawns and his lack of attention to her subsequent remarks, which he imperfectly concealed. She thought him fatigued like herself, and suggested they retire to their separate rooms to nap, instead of going out to watch the May dances which apparently were going to occur. He lay down then on his old bed and went immediately to sleep and did not wake until just before dinnertime.

For a moment when he woke, he could not remember where he was or what he was there for. The sight of his valise brought him back to the present situation. "Well," he thought to himself, "the time is getting on. I must either be about it, and finish it, or yield the lovely money and go back to London." Nevertheless he lingered over dinner and surprised his mother by his interest in their company.

"If you do not leave, Bysshe," his father said with asperity, "we might have had our dinner at our usual hour."

"I like your wine, sire," his son answered him obliquely. "I'll have more of it if I may."

His father did not refuse him, but he commented: "You will find yourself in the ditch, if you continue in this vein and drive back tonight. And I wish you may."

The light was fading. The Marquis could see it drawing away from the far-off fields and hills, through the windows where the curtains had not been drawn. He sighed under his breath, slightly, and stood up, and asked for his horses to be brought out. He much regretted the absence of his valet, but he managed to exchange his gold coat and his heavily laced shirt for his travelling coat and a plainer shirt. He put his small valise, with the articles he had collected, in his curricle, saluted his mother, smiled rather wistfully at his father, and left as the dark was falling. But his spirits quickened as he left the constraints of his father's house, and felt the night wind rising against his face. He forgot the past hours, and bent all his considerable attention on his adventure.

III

THE RAPE

The Marquis drove first to the crossing where the London road and the long road to Rotherby met, and there he guided the curricle a little way into the woods until he judged it out of sight of any curious passer-by. He transferred the coiled ladder to his saddle, the domino to his pocket, and tethered one horse. The other he mounted, and set off on a steady pace across the fields, not so fast as in the day, but he knew them well. He judged he should arrive a little before eleven, when the house, keeping country hours, weary after the Hunt and readying for the journey back to London, should be in deepest sleep; and so he did. Suddenly the great house loomed ahead. He stopped his horse long before the sound of any whinnying noise could be heard, tied and hobbled her, and taking his ladder under his riding cape, he walked boldly across the lawn.

He had decided that if he were seen, he would know how to make a good story, and that would end his venture. But the house was dark, the moon not yet up above the trees, and casting patterned shadows in which he could walk, hardly visible even to a watcher, had there been one. There were no eyes, the house was fast asleep. He came to the tree, and climbed the level boughs of the beech, a smooth ladder, and made the little jump to the stony balcony. The night was fresh, the day had been warm—the windows were ajar. He smiled at this trustingness in country virtue, and wondered if he would find Cressida in the bed, or some other guest, or one of her brothers. On this chance remembrance his success he knew would lie. He had no way in so short a time to check that would not have made his interest known. Even in the soft night dark he could see that he had hit a woman's room. He knotted the rope ladder to a baluster of the balcony, and stepped inside.

The room was darker than the outside air. The Marquis paused, letting his breathing quieten, and his eyes, like a cat's, grow used to the dark. Then he slipped his mask on, and took one of the several handkerchiefs he had brought with him out of his pocket and held it loosely in his hand. He had not many choices. He could throttle the sleeping girl, but that did not appeal to him, or hit her hard, nor did that appeal more. But somehow he had the problem of simultaneously waking her and silencing any cry. He could not risk even a little noise, he knew, and certainly not a scream. He walked soundlessly to the bed, looked at the girl who lay there, sleeping deeply, recognised her. He stood for a moment, surveying her askance, not risking an intensity of gaze to waken her.

The Rape

No pity moved him, no compunction, no regret—only an interest, impersonal, considering. He really did not want to hurt or terrify her more than absolutely he had to, for it was his intention, if he could, to seduce, not rape her, but that, taking time, could not possibly be done here in her room. He could press a pillow on her face, but that struck him as grotesque, and possibly injurious, and also her head was nestled on the only one. He was well-armed, a small knife in his pocket and his smallest pistol, and of course his light sword, but she might scream first, and anyway he knew he would not use them. His first idea still seemed best to him. Her lips were faintly parted as she breathed. He bent down and forced the handkerchief whole and roughly into her mouth and held it there with one hand, and quick like a cat, at almost the same second, had thrown his whole weight on her. He saw her eyes fly open, and her body moved slightly beneath him, but his weight and his hand held her firm.

So far, so good, he thought. "Lie still," he whispered, "and I'll not hurt you now. Move and I will." He was not sure she heard him, or understood him, and he took no chances on it. Carefully he took a handkerchief he had stuffed at the top of his coat for this purpose, and with a swift movement, wrapped it around her mouth and head and knotted it. Her big eyes stared at him piteously in bewildered terror, but she could not even whimper. That secured, the rest was not so difficult. He sat up on top of her holding her body still paralysed between his knees, and drew her wrists together and knotted them in front of her with one of the several handkerchiefs remaining in his pocket; then he did the same to her knees, and finally her ankles. "I have you, as you see," he said in a menacing whisper. "Lie still, and I'll not kill you." He showed her his knife and his pistol to awe her, and promised to knock her with his fist if she kicked him. Suddenly remembering how well she knew the countryside, he took out his last handkerchief and bandaged her eyes with it. Then he lifted her and slung her over his shoulder, and crossed quickly on noiseless feet to the door and locked it. He arranged the bed coverings and the pillow to look to a casual glance as if she still slept, for another precaution just in case, and made his way softly with her to the window and out into the air.

Here the Marquis stopped, and let her down so that she faced him, and slipped her arms over his head, about his neck. Then cautiously, holding her in front of him, with one arm he descended the ladder. He was strong, for besides riding and fencing, he worked out regularly in the boxing gyms, but he found this abduction business a difficult and awkward affair. Once down, he slung her, sack-style, again over his shoulder. She lay so limp, he was surprised at her lack of spirit, forgetting the force of his grim threats, and he wondered if she had fainted. The moon was up now, but no one saw him stride across the lawn. He threw her up onto the saddle, across it, and mounted behind her. It was not a romantic position, but he had neither romantic feelings nor aims. She stirred uncomfortably once or twice, apparently having come round, if she had fainted. He checked the pace of his horse, and shifted her into one arm, as he would have carried a little child. Another man might have felt touched at the feel of her head curled against him, helpless and oddly enough, in its limpness, even trusting, but certainly he did not. Had he been capable of it, he would not have started on such a sport. Business, he would rather have put it, for in so cold and careful a light he regarded it.

In due time he reached the curricle, but he did not stop there. Instead he rode on, by a short route he knew, into the low hills and the hollow he had marked out. Once there, he dismounted, his eyes glittering behind his mask, a black shape in the faint moonlight. Estimating the time, he could allow two hours, he thought, if need be, for this business and the getting her back into her bed, if he was to make London and the hell before morning. He was a man of considerable energy and few doubts. Picking up the helpless girl, he strode with her to the impromptu bed of bearskin rugs and furs he had made and laid her down. She was shivering, perhaps with shock, perhaps with fear, certainly from the night air in her thin gown. He tucked the furs up well around her, removing the bandage from her eyes as he bent over her, and then stood looking down at her. Her eyes looked back at him above the handkerchief's edge with a certain fearlessness that surprised him, but no other emotion that he could read.

"You will wonder why I have brought you here," he said in a level voice, "and I will tell you. I intend to rape you." At the faint start she made, he frowned, and continued. "You are miles away from any house, or any road, or anyone who could hear you, scream you never so loud or long. Do you understand me? There is no one, absolutely no one, who can hear you who will come to your aid—and there is nothing, absolutely nothing, that can prevent my doing to you exactly what I fully mean to do. I have brought you here to do it, and never doubt I shall. Put all hopes of that aside." He studied her face, but could read no response there, except a sort of bewilderment. He continued, less fiercely: "But how I go about it can be in large part your decision. There's just you and I, and if there's no one here to help, there's also no one here to watch or know how it is done." He paused. "Now if your pride, your virtue, honour, whatever you want to call the thing, demands a forcible rape, I can oblige you. It will be quick, and that would rather suit me, but I warn you frankly you will find it rather shattering and it will frankly hurt." Then he smiled grimly and briefly. "Nor is it my way. I have made love to many women, to our mutual delights, and I have never made a forcible rape. But I daresay there can be a first. That, I said, is up to you. Shall we discuss it? I will take my lovely handkerchief from your mouth, it is a very good silk and clean but I daresay unpleasant and uncomfortable—but you must promise me that you'll not scream or shriek or make any loud noises. Not because I'm worried anyone else will hear, just because it's late and I don't want to. And I don't have to—it can stay. Choose now, this first. You only have to turn your head to show that you'll be quiet and I'll take the thing away. If we come to no agreement, I can always put it back."

He was pleased to see that she did as he suggested. He knelt down beside her and gently untied the tight knot and fished out the damp rag, and laid his finger on her lips in a warning. "But don't ask me why, for I'll not tell you. And don't waste your breath appealing to me, I am told I am incorrigible. I have been told so just today." She moved her dry lips, but she made no attempt to cry or speak. Her stillness surprised him. She reminded him of a verse he had heard that morning, "As the lamb before the slaughterer is dumb," but he put the recollection from him.

"Now, that's better. I can see you, what this moon allows, though that's not very much. Now, my dear, your case is very bad, and there's no help for that. I am said to be a rather winning lover, so they tell me, but I know that you don't want me. But since you really have no choice about it, why not see what I can do to make the night as little bad as it need be? But I don't want to have to go pursuing you and running round the woods after you. I'd get you back, but I'd lose my temper and time both. Promise me you'll stay right here, and do your best to lie still, and I'll unbind you." He looked at her. "That is all you have to do. The rest is up to me."

"What will you do if I don't promise?" she asked faintly, so that he had to bend to catch her words. His face grew rather cold, and he stood up, akimbo.

"I will stake your legs and arms apart, so, to keep them out of my way, and stick my handkerchief back in your mouth, and despatch the matter, now."

He seemed in earnest, incredible though it appeared. Her face looked frightened and drawn. "And what if I do promise?" He bent again to catch her words. "Will you wait a little—have you time?"

His face softened. "I think that you are truly frightened."

"I am so afraid," she said in despair.

"Afraid, perhaps—why *so* afraid?"

"I do not know at all what all this means or what you mean to do to me," she said, very low.

He was briefly nonplussed, and then he laughed, and sat down conversationally beside her. He put his hand on her bound ones. "My dear," he said, "if you will promise as I ask, I promise you I'll never speak of how I did this act, whatever it may be. You can say, if you like, that you were tied and kicked me hard and screamed and finally in the end I put you out with drugs. And that way can be done, of course. But if you promise me, I'll treat you like a dearest friend. We'll sit awhile together here, and talk and count the stars and make acquaintanceship a bit. We'll play at being lovers here."

"I think then I must promise you; the other would be foolish," she said with a little sigh.

"Smart girl," he said, and lightly kissed her hair. A shudder shook her, even at the light touch, profoundly. He pulled the rugs back and untied his handkerchiefs from her wrists and knees and feet, and covered her back up. Then, as if to test her promise and her resolve, he walked a little away, but she did not move.

"I woke you in the middle of the night," he said surprisingly. "You will want to excuse yourself. Go a little off, I will turn my back, but don't run off. I don't give or accept promises very often, but when I do, I mean them kept. I should quickly catch you, and make you wish you hadn't."

"You are considerate," she said between stiff lips that wanted to tremble, wondering if he were mad, but she availed herself of his permission. She came back as she promised, but as she neared the pile of rugs she halted, afraid to run from his looming figure, but unable to make herself move towards him. She stood there, in her light gown, her undressed hair gleaming and tumbling about her shoulders. He watched her dispassionately, then he walked forward and put his hand on her arm. She caught her breath as his shadow fell on her, but she did not resist him and mutely let him lead her again to his impromptu couch, where he pulled the top rug back for her and then covered her with it once more. He walked to the other side and directed a glance at her, but she had shut her eyes and lay as if asleep. He removed his coat and neckcloth, his shoes, and his breeches, pulled his side of the rug back and slipped under himself.

At first he stayed some inches from her, making no move to touch her, talking gently to her, mainly nonsense. Then after a while he put a folded rug under his head, and reaching out, gathered her into the fold of his arms, and lay there breathing quietly, holding her lightly. At that moment, since he felt not the slightest desire for her, his presence was infinitely restful in the quiet night. She did not need to know his name to feel his strength and his authority and despite his evident brutality, the oddly gentle quality of his nature that did not show itself except at moments such as this. Although reason would have told her still to be afraid, these things had their way and gentled her, until her heart stilled, and she rested quietly, even drowsily in his arms on his breast, as though he were her father or her brother, she thought, except, she thought, "I'd never be like this with them"—or as if they had been lovers for many years. He showed her the patterns on the moon, and what stars could be seen, still in its haze, and which planets had been out—described the little animals that were about them in the woods—chatted lazily about this and that, though carefully never about persons or events. Years later, she thought to her surprise, she might name these moments as among the most peaceful and most pleasant she would spend. They stretched so calmly, in that still cool light of May as if they had no beginning and would have no ending, but such feelings are only feelings, and of course, in time these moments ended. She sensed his change of mood, his purpose gathering itself, and her body tensed itself and her heart began to beat furiously.

"The main thing frightening you, my dear," he said, resting his fingers lightly on her heart, "is ignorance, I think. Let's see why that should be. You can fear me, yes, but not excessively —and out here, on this hill or in a marriage bed, I'm just a man. No monster or no hero."

She did not answer him, but her trembling increased. He touched a beating pulse in her wrist, then he stroked her hair, and said, "Does that frighten you?"

She shook her head. "Does it please you?" She shook her head. He laughed a bit, and then he lightly kissed her on the forehead. "Does that frighten you?" She shook her head. He kissed lightly her eyebrows, then her eyes, her nose, the tips of her ears, the surface of her lips, her chin, light butterfly kisses. Then her neck, more hungeringly, and the hollow of her throat, and then returning to her lips, he forced them just a bit apart. They did not respond, and he could feel them trying to withdraw.

"So much for that," he said lightly, leaning on his elbow. "We must try something else. With you, my dear, *c'est plus difficile.*" He sat up and looked at her. "Cressy, do you know *at all* what men and women do?"

She shook her head and did not look at him, nor did she show surprise at his use of her name.

"But you do know how animals are made, no?"

"We have horses," she faltered, "and other animals, at Rotherby."

"C' n'est pas presqu' la même chose," he murmured, "but it will do. Perhaps you've seen them mating?"

4 6

"No, monsieur," she answered quietly. He sighed.

"You have brothers. Have you seen them?"

"Monsieur?"

"Naked, I mean? In the bath? When you were children?"

She shook her head. "They were older than I was. And we had a governess."

"They never got you off alone?"

"Monsieur!"

"Some boys or brothers do. They're curious, too." He tried again. "Did you ever come upon your father unawares? Undressed, I mean?"

"No, never." He sighed in exasperation.

"Tales in school, perhaps, or other girls?" He shook his head. "No, I see, not you." He paused and was silent a moment. "The bulge men have in front, beneath our breeches. That's my point. Have you ever thought about it? What it is there for? How it's used? No questions ever?"

"My mother died, monsieur," she said, with simple dignity. "I never asked—my father."

"Well, now you're going to know. And by God, I'd say it's time." She began to shake again. He looked at her curiously. "Poor Cressy," he said softly, "poor innocent. Perfect knowledge, so they say, casts out fear." She looked at him wonderingly. He put his finger on her lips, and said, "Now, my dear—" he paused, searching—*"Je voudrais expliquer tous ce que je veux faire. Au fin, ça ira mieux, je crois.* It is a matter of conception we're about. You know the word? It's in the Prayer Book, lamb, you've heard it every Christmas. 'A virgin conceived.' Didn't you wonder what that meant?"

"I know these things in general only. My father said there would be time—" Her voice broke.

"Ah, so you *have* asked?" She did not answer. "Have you ever liked a man?" he asked suddenly and abruptly.

"I—I do not know."

"Won't say?" His swift changes between a kind of tenderness and hammer blows bewildered and unnerved her. "Had kisses stolen at a ball, perhaps, some little room?" She shook her head. "Twenty-two, and yet a mere *enfant*, who nothing knows. So I had heard. A citadel indeed. That makes it hard, but—" His voice lost its musing tone. "Very well, *enfant*, then we begin."

The Marquis disengaged himself from the fur that covered them, and stood up, his legs apart, as if astride, wearing only his shirt, his stockings down. "You, *regarde-moi.*" Her eyes were shut, her face turned away. "Look at me, I said. Looking will not hurt." Reluctantly, drawn by the sternness in his voice, she turned her face and opened her eyes, for a moment, towards where he stood, his face shadowed, but his shirt and limbs silvered and white in the faint moonlight, then she shut her eyes quickly with an invisible flush. "Again, my dear. Stare all you like. I do not mind. That's all there is." Then he came back into the shadows, close to her, on one knee beside her, on the furry skin. "Put out your hand, my dear, lay it in mine. Now touch me here." She drew back her hand as if burned, but he did not let it go and drew it out again firmly, his fingers like steel talons on hers. "Do as I say. Feel me," he said, guiding her hand and fingers slowly. "Imagine you are blind, discover what it's like by touch alone. That's better now. A little thing, you see, nothing to fear. Hold it in your hand, so." Suddenly she wrenched her hand away, and he gave a little gasp, and his own hand shook on hers. "Oh, lord, this moves too quick! That change, my dear, is what we mean by 'love.' You did not know. Put your hand back. That is the most you have to fear, is it so fearsome? Now we must make you ready, dear, so it won't hurt."

He slid back under the rug beside her, and gently lifted her skirt above her belly. She stiffened and would have drawn away, but he held her with his arm and reminded her of her promise. "Be easy, love, take a breath, lie easy and forget me and let me work." He massaged her small belly gently for a time, his roaming hands and long fingers going sometimes above, sometimes just below, then moved up to her breasts, small like the rest of her, and gently slid her thin nightgown over them and kissed them, taking a nipple in his teeth. " 'License my roving hands,' " he said huskily, " 'and let them go—around—behind—above—below.' " She gave a little cry, but he pressed his lips briefly on hers. "I shall not hurt, my dear. This frightens you, I know that it is very strange, but it is meant to be, we all are made to do it, you as well as any other. There is a place, and we will find it, where I am meant to be. Relax, my dear." She moaned and twisted beneath him, but he would not stop or take his fingers from her, and gradually, as the moments went by, she stopped her ineffectual struggles and her thighs began to loosen and to part. She hardly knew when he exchanged himself for his fingers, only his hands were now about her, behind her back, lifting her, his lips on hers, his tongue exploring the cavities of her mouth. Her moans were lost in his breath. When his gentleness turned to violence, his chest and lips smothered her panting cries, and then he himself gave a great cry, and clasped her hard to him. "I am dying," she thought and tightened her

arms about him and kissed him in return. "Oh my dear, my
dear, my dear," he said and kissed her eyelids and clasped her
again convulsively. They lay so for some time, his weight
pressing her down. She could not move. Then gradually the
strange fullness within her slid away, and after a bit he rolled
from her. He crossed her legs and thighs over each other, why
she did not know, and lay resting on his back. He did not
speak, and she did not move. Her helpless thoughts seemed to
have left her, she could not summon any, and so she lay still,
not moving, under the skins, and waited. Suddenly, all at
once, he raised himself on an elbow, and looked down at her
and smiled. "Well, that's all there is, my dear.—No more than
that. Now you know. Your husband should be grateful to me,
when he does arrive." She did not speak. "Stay there," he
cautioned her, and getting up, walked a little away. When he
came back, he had clothed himself again, and carried the
small flask.

"Drink this, my dear," he said.

She cried out in fright then: "Oh, sir, I've done what you
demanded. You will not kill me now, oh please, don't murder
me!"

He looked at her without expression. "No Lucretia, then?"
She only stared at him, her eyes wide and panic-stricken.
"Lucretia killed herself when this was done to her, with her
own hands." She lay, terrified, and he took pity on her. "It's
not what you think, my dear, it's just a sleeping draught to
help me get you back again, quietly, and so that I won't have
to leave you tied. Drink it now." He held it to her lips. She
put her hands on his wrist, futilely trying to push him away.

"I see you don't believe me," he said. "That's a pity, for

you'll have to drink it anyway. Good lord, chit, why should I poison you, that would cause a *devil* of a stir! It won't even make you drunk. Drink now." She pushed against him hopelessly, twisting her head away, but he held her with his weight, and pushed it brutally between her clenched teeth and held it, forcing back her head. Even so, she would not swallow, until losing patience, he slapped her cheeks sharply. She lost her breath, gasped, and as he relentlessly pressed the flask against her inner throat, swallowed once, and choking at the bitter taste, she did as he desired and drank it all. This final humiliation overcame her, and she began to cry, almost soundlessly, her body shaking.

"My lord, poor chit!" he said. "This was too much." He pulled her nightgown over her, and tucked the bear rug warmly round her, his riding cloak over himself. "I'll stay here till you go to sleep. Poor girl, I haven't murdered you, believe me; in the morning you'll wake up, don't be afraid. But this way is better for us both." He looked at her sternly. "It's too late now for vapours. If you don't be still yourself, I'll make you drink my brandy, and that will calm you."

"I c-c-can't, my lord."

"*What* did you say?" he asked, startled.

"Monsieur, I think I'd like your brandy." He strode over to his things and came back with his own flask. She drank several sips, gasping at the fiery taste, and closed her eyes. He stroked her hair, and murmured little comforts. Gradually, her shuddering ceased.

"Why did you say, 'my lord'?" he asked softly, more casually than he felt, when he saw she was lying quiet.

"That's what you've been to me tonight, I think," she answered faintly, half asleep. A few minutes later, he saw that she had fallen asleep under the effect of his mother's laudanum.

The night was slipping away. He rose, considering how best to use it. He put his cloak on the ground, and carried her onto it, then rolled up the skins and tied them, bulkily, behind his saddle. His handkerchiefs he put back in his pockets, all except one with which he rebandaged her eyes, and put on his coat. His domino he left on still, for although he did not think that she would wake, he thought to take no risks. He lifted her in his cloak on the saddle, and looked about and saw nothing left. Then he mounted behind her, laid her within the circle of one arm, and rode with all possible haste back to the curricle. His second horse was standing patiently, as he had left it. He unloaded the rugs and skins, and then able to travel more conveniently, continued on to Rotherby. He thought the time must be nearing three.

The house was as still as before. He made his way quickly this time back up the ladder, the girl lying limp on his shoulder. He carried her into her room and laid her down on her bed, and stood thinking. He looked about the room and saw a stand of drawers. He walked over to it swiftly, and opened first one and then the other, until he found what he wanted. Returning to the bed, he raised her up and slipped her nightgown off over her head, and slipped the fresh one on, without a glance to spare for her person. He laid her back down, and covered her with the sheet, then folded the nightgown she had worn carefully and put it in his coat. He frowned and thought again, and taking out his knife, he cut a long lock of her hair from underneath where the loss would be least likely to be noticed, wrapped it in his own handkerchief and placed it in his inner coat pocket. He saw nothing more to serve his purpose and left the room, closing the windows just ajar as he had found them. He pulled up the ladder, unknotted it, tied it again about his waist, and swung lightly back into the beech tree and climbed nimbly down. Taking off his mask, he strolled casually across the lawn, took horse again and rode back first to his curricle, then drove at great speed to London.

The dawn was coming as he drove up before the hell, but some lights, he thought, still burned behind the heavy curtains. His friends looked up with languid surprise as he appeared, caped and spurred, in the door. They laid down their cards.

"B'Jove, I didn't really think to see you," said the Honourable Frederic, a faint curiosity on his face. "Did you really do the chit?"

The Marquis looked at him with something like disgust, and did not answer. He strode over to where the Viscount Lisle was lounging and produced, first the cut lock of hair in its distinctive colour, and then the nightgown with its embroidered letters on the neck and the slight stains and scents of the night.

"*Le vrai* red gold, *ça*," commented the Viscount Rockfort admiringly. "One seldom sees it. An enviable drawing. Gore, I felicitate you." The Marquis smiled briefly.

"Speaking evidence, indeed," the Viscount Lisle murmured. "I'd say that Gore collects, at least on the first." He opened his box, passed part of the money across. He smiled, and added: "Tomorrow, we'll see what comes of it."

"I shall take all, I think," the Marquis said. The Viscount reached across to take the articles, to put them in his box, but the Marquis intervened.

"I think not," he said, drawing his light sword. Picking up the two on its point, he carried them delicately across the room and deposited both on the embers of the fire. The other four watched with interest, particularly the young Viscount Teviot, who was sitting nearest to the fire. The Marquis stared at them silently, until they flamed and burned away. Then he yawned, and said to Teviot: "No cards for me. I'm demned tired; I'm off to bed." He tapped the Honourable Frederic on the head as he went by with the sword which he still held. "Over to you, Lord Herriot, the next turn's yours. And by the by, give me the doubling of my stake."

"Double my stakes as well?" said the Honourable Frederic, rather gloomily, handing it over. "Same stakes, same odds?"

"If you like," said the Marquis obliquely. "You won't collect, I think." He bowed and took his leave, went home, unpacked his gear, and fell into an undisturbed sleep.

IV

THE INFORMING

But if the Marquis was able to sleep soundly, the Viscount Teviot was not. The game had suddenly changed its face, and turned to earnest, for he had recognised the owner of the Marquis' trophies. He was himself a cousin of Cressy's, though several removes distant, and had liked her very much; in fact, at one time he had fancied himself in love, though she had never known it. His emotions in a turmoil, he had excused himself shortly after the Marquis left, and walked home, trying to think. His brains were in poor condition for thinking, and he could not sort out his conflicting claims.

His first thought was to call the Marquis out, but on second thought he could not see the good of it to Cressy. The Marquis, being the better sword and the better pistol, would undoubtedly put a quick and furious end to his suspicions and himself. He placed no reliance on heaven's intervention; and in any case the merits of his cause were mixed. Gore would have a point, he thought, for he had been for the game himself, and they had all agreed to it, and if by some miracle Gore was kept from calling him out, one of the others might. It was a dreadful tangle, he thought.

He considered hiring a messenger to go to his relative, Lord Salisbury, but then the messenger could in the end be traced back to him, and he did not doubt the Duke would do it. And suppose the message went astray. That did not bear thinking on. He considered going to Lord Salisbury himself and making a clean breast of the whole matter, but his courage failed him at the thought of what his Grace would have to say. He could not face the scene. Salisbury would despise him, his friends would despise him, the ton would despise him, and he, who had really done very little, just acquiesced, would be ruined more than the wicked Gore or anyone—not only a rake but a dishonourable informer. Nevertheless, he could not put the matter from him. He knew Cressy well, he thought her a sweet, ordinary girl, and the whole business suddenly sickened him, as it had not when some mythical unknown excitement, some unreal shocking adventure, was the idea. He was younger, and less hardened than his peers. He could not solve his problem, and finally went to sleep.

He awoke some hours later, still troubled, but with his head clearer. No one, he realised suddenly, had any idea that he had recognised who the things belonged to. They could not blame him, since they did not know. He would muffle himself in a heavy coat and scarf, in the evening, and incognito, pretending not to be himself, he would hand a note to the foot-

man at the door of the house to give to Lord Salisbury. Then
he would have done his duty by his cousin, her father could do
the rest, whatever that might be, and no one need know his
part. He breathed a sigh of relief, and turned his attention to
the composing of the note.

After several attempts which he discarded, he wrote:

"Ask your daughter why the Lord Gore boasts to have your
daughter's initialled nightrail and a lock of her hair in his
possession. A Well-Wisher."

They might think it was a servant, he thought. They might
think what they liked, for all he cared. He wished it were dark
already, he wished he had done it and could forget it. He saw
no honour in the sending of a sneak note, but then he did not
see much honour in the business anywhere. Accordingly,
suitably muffled, he presented himself at eight, at Lord Salisbury's town house, to be told his Grace had not yet come up
from the country. He was chagrined. If the chit was in the
country, he did not see how Gore had managed it. He thought
perhaps that it was he who had been mistaken. But the footman had the note, and he did not like to ask for it back. Had
he been drunk and imagined it all? Then Lord Salisbury
would find it all a mistake, and that would end it. But if his
daughter had already told him, then he would know for certain with whom he had to deal. With these reflections the
Viscount had to be content, and resuming his proper appearance, he went on first to his Coffee House, and then to the
hell, where he found three of his friends playing in their usual
way.

The Honourable Frederic came in after a bit, and said his
assignment had gone out of town. He looked somewhat em-

barrassed, and then he said, in a rush: "Stab me, Bysshe, but you know, I haven't got the nerve. I'll just pay my stake." The Viscount who had proposed the game rose courteously, and said that he would try his hand, and left the room. The others did not look up. The Marquis was somewhat drunker than his usual state, but otherwise he seemed his cool, undisturbed self.

The Viscount Rockfort, lifting his eyes from his cards, said wickedly: "Perhaps Lord Gore would bring her here for you. Then maybe you would find your nerve?"

"I might," the Honourable Frederic said. "It's worth the try. Gore, would you do it?"

"No, I wouldn't," said Lord Gore, his attention on his cards. "The once is quite enough for me, I do assure you. Not my style. Anyway, they don't let women in a hell."

"Bring her in as a page," said the Honourable Frederic, guffawing. "That would be a sport."

The Marquis, having just won the bank, without answering suddenly rose, and took his winnings and left, remarking he was expected at his cousin's ball.

V

THE AWAKENING

Lord Salisbury and his family did not arrive in London until nine that same night. They had started late. The Duke had found that he had various matters on his estate, after the Hunt, to attend to unexpectedly. He and his sons were gone most of the day, checking which walls required mending, and the condition of the hunters. They left early and came back only briefly for lunch, and they had no time to send more than a glance towards Cressy. She had slept late, much later than her custom, until ten, but her abigail, finding the door locked, saw no reason to disturb her, glad of a longer time for her own affairs.

The sun filled Cressy's room, through the windows still ajar, and fell across her face. When she woke, at first she did not remember. Her thoughts were pleasantly disconcerned, and her limbs relaxed, still from the drug's effect. Then quite clearly she did remember. She put her fingers over her lips in a frightened way and lay still and wondered what would happen, if she moved, and wondered what to do. She could not tell her father. She saw that. It was already late in the morning, and day had well begun. She could not imagine herself walking into her father's study and announcing her new estate. She would not know how to begin. She stretched and moved her limbs and discovered that she really was not hurt, she was much herself. In the light of her present safety, after her terrible fears, thinking of what was past seemed unwise. Perhaps if she were quiet, things would go on as they had before. Her mind would go no further than that. She had been given too much to think about and to feel at once, and so she ended by thinking of nothing.

After a time, she thought she must get up. She noticed her gown had been changed, and that surprised and troubled her, and made her flush. She could not find the other, and that worried her. She could imagine no reason why it should be gone, and no way but one. The problem was too much for her, and she abandoned it. She walked rather awkwardly and gingerly to the door and found it locked and flushed again at yet another reminder. She wished to have a bath brought up, and called her abigail. After she had bathed and dressed and breakfasted downstairs, she felt much better. The discovery later of the missing lock of hair while her hair was being dressed filled her with a terrible foreboding, for she could think of many reasons why it should be taken, and how it could be used, and none reassuring. She thought then: "I must tell my father. There is no other way." But she had so little to tell. After coffee, and a walk about the garden, she again felt so much better that she found herself most comfortable putting it from her mind, and concentrating on the things that needed attention before they left.

If she was quiet and heavy-lidded over lunch, her busy men had no leisure to observe it. If she was more silent than her custom in the coach and over dinner, as they drove up, since her brothers rode outside all the way and her father most of it, they thought her merely tired and were solicitous but unconcerned. She had no wish to enlighten them. Their ignorant unconcern soothed her. It was therefore with incredulous shock that his Grace read his billet through, late that night, after Cressy had retired, and he had seen to other businesses in his house and set in motion the preparations for the coming rout.

It was written on plain paper, he noted, but not by an uneducated hand. He read it through again, casting his eye back onto his daughter's actions in the day, and realised he had seen little of her. He could make nothing of it that way. Such violent anger swept over him that he wanted to break the ornaments on his desk, to rage and storm about the room, but he did neither. Instead, he sat thoughtfully at his desk, considering. He wished he could simply throw the note away, in the end, and for a moment he was tempted to do so, but only for a moment. His first impulse had not been to shrug it off, why he did not know. But until morning he could not see what he could do. On impulse, late as it was, he sent a messenger to learn if Lord Gore had visited his father the weekend past.

When morning came, at a time when he knew Cressy was

occupied downstairs, he took her abigail and went to his daughter's room. He had the abigail look through her drawers. He wanted to make her a present, he said, for a surprise, of a new nightrobe. He was looking, he said, to see if she did not have one of the new initialled kind. The abigail informed him that her mistress indeed had one, but she herself did not find it, and she had missed it down at Rotherby when she packed the day before, but her mistress had said she had thought it would be here. In that case, the Duke said, he would certainly procure her another in its place, and it must be kept a surprise. He knew his interest might be thought unusual, but he also knew the abigail entertained few thoughts of any sort.

Later in the morning, he called Cressy to speak with him in his private study. She stood before him, in her morning gown of muslin, much the same, except he noticed now the shadows under her eyes, as if she had not slept well, and he wondered. He asked her if she was happy over their entertainment for the evening, and she said she was. When he taxed her with a lack of cheerfulness, she only smiled at him and said she was a little tired. He had her take a chair beside him, and ruffled his fingers through her bright hair, as he often did.

"Don't muss me, sir," she said smiling, "or I shall look a fright!"

Suddenly his fingers found what they had been searching out. "What's this, missy?" he said. "Have you been cutting off your hair?" She flushed and looked uncomfortable, and he hoped she would speak; but then she smiled a little, and only said she had gotten such a tangle in the Hunt, she had snipped it off and hoped it would not show. With that he had to be content. Like his daughter, he felt he could not bring himself to face the subject with her, especially since he saw she had no intention of confiding in him. But his heart swelled with love and anger, and he watched her narrowly as she walked from the room. On an impulse he rose and called her back, and took her hands, and said in his tenderest voice: "Cressy, what's troubling you? Won't you tell me?" He saw her eyes suddenly grow bright with tears, but she did not tell him anything.

Meanwhile, the preparations for the rout went on. Catering and decorating occupied the household. Cressy had had her gown and its accessories in order since the week before, and so she was free to attend to directing with the servants the matters of the house. She had been very excited the week before, but now she had to pull herself through the day. She was glad when afternoon came and she had an excuse to retire to rest. She knew very well her strange companion had been a man, if not of her set, of her world. She could not mistake the signs, and what had made the night easier to bear was the harder now, because it showed what little value one who knew her had placed upon her. It was a bitter knowledge, and she could find no sense in it. She could hardly bear the thought of such a one observing her, without her knowing, perhaps even in her house that night. Nevertheless, she resolved to conduct herself as usual. She saw nothing else to do.

While she rested, her father closeted himself with her brothers, Kittredge and Timothy. After some deliberation he had decided to share his suspicions with them. They stood in the middle of the room, slightly lounging, tall, for the Hunt rather than for the ton, twins with the same hair as their sister. He began without preamble: "What would you say if I told you a town buck had gotten your sister's honour?"

"I'd say it was a poor joke; and I would not laugh much," said Kit, as he was called. He had preceded his brother by a short time into the world, and as the heir, had the more gravity.

"In bad taste, not your style," explained Timothy irrepressibly, undeterred by his father's looks, "and also not possible."

"Nevertheless, it would seem to be the case," the Duke replied. Their eyes narrowed, and their attention sharpened. They stopped lounging, and came over to him.

"Who told you?" Kit asked for them both.

"A well-wisher," he said, and his lips curled with distaste. He showed them the note.

"Do you believe this muck?" Kit asked incredulously. "We know the Marquis. He's a little wild but not the sort to do a game like this. And he knows Cressy too, at least he knows she is our sister." He dropped the note in disgust. "I don't believe this."

"No more did I, at first," the Duke said carefully.

"Bysshe has fallen in with several friends I could believe it of," said Timothy, "—Rockfort and the Viscount Lisle. But I don't see the point."

"I do not see it either," said the Duke. "Nevertheless, if it is true, and I think it is, the Marquis shall feel mine." He looked at them. "She does not want to talk to me. Go find your sister, and make some excuse to stay with her awhile. Talk to her naturally, and observe her now, and then come back to me and tell me what you think."

After an hour, they came back, somewhat subdued. Kit was of two minds still, but Timothy said: "I think it may be true. She's not the same; she has something on her mind. I last really saw her Saturday, at the Hunt, and she has changed too much." His habitual good humour had left his eyes.

Kit, cautious, said: "What of the articles the note referred to?"

"I could find neither," his Grace said dryly, "and I do not believe that they were given willingly."

"Well, why don't she just tell you?" asked Timothy explosively.

His Grace shook his head. "She may yet. She will be ashamed."

Kit, still unbelieving, asked: "When was it done? The Marquis was not at the Hunt."

"No," the Duke agreed. "But he was at his father's house." He saw the point was not lost on them.

"Lord!" exclaimed Timothy, shocked. "He never goes there. They do not get along."

"I thought it interesting," commented the Duke, watching them behind veiled eyelids.

"How could you know it?" exploded the older twin.

"I sent to learn," his father replied briefly.

"What shall we do?" asked Timothy. "Shall we call him out?"

"I shall kill him," said Kit. "I thought he was a friend."

"Kill him?" said the Duke thoughtfully. "I do not think so."

"Then tell us," they said. "We will do what you direct."

They were as outraged finally as he could have wished, for

she was their younger only sister, and they had adored her always, and she them, even when they teased her. They might annoy her themselves, but no one else might, and they had always rallied strongly to her. So now they did. They knew several stories they had heard of the Marquis in recent years with which they enlightened their father, and lessened his surprise at the Marquis' name appearing in the note.

The social affair that was planned for that night was opportune, the Duke of Salisbury considered. The families of Adversane and Salisbury no longer met, except at the larger gatherings, but he believed the Marquis' and his family's names had both been on his secretary's list. The Duke and Duchess he did not expect, for they rarely came up to town. The Marquis might yet come, he thought. With his sons he planned what reception they would together make for him, should he make an appearance.

THE TAKING

The Marquis had forgotten the invitation, but as he looked through his cards for the week, his valet reminded him. "Oh, lord," he said, "I suppose I must go." It did not enter his mind that it might be dangerous for him to go, and his pride somewhat required it. His mind was occupied with a race he had planned with Lord Lynton on the Wednesday, and the events of the weekend had faded.

"I think you must, my lord," his valet said. "This is his Grace's yearly rout. Will your father journey up?"

"I think not," said the Marquis absently. "I wonder if it's not too late to go? What time did it begin?" He rightly guessed, since nothing in two days had happened, that Cressy had kept her secrets to herself. It might amuse him, after all, to go, though he would keep his distance from her. He supposed she would appear. "What coat, Robertson, shall I wear?"

"The blue and silver was delivered today," his valet suggested. "It should show your lordship to a good advantage."

"As you like," the Marquis said, "but I want the Brussels lace." His valet looked surprised at this unusual interest. The Marquis, for reasons of his own, thought a delicate-appearing wrist might be tactful.

"Do you dine here, my lord?"

"I haven't time. I'll dine out afterwards." He gave his thought entirely over to his clothes.

Even omitting dinner, he arrived late. His host was not in sight, but he saw friends of his near the entrance to the drawing room, and stood talking with them there. He saw his host's daughter at the other end of the long salon, both herself and her reflection in the glass, though she was turned away from him. She was in a white dress, with lace at her elbows, falling over her arms in a way that caught his eye as most graceful. She was laughing with a school friend of his, John Neville, and he felt a sudden impulse to join them, and see her face to face, but common sense held him where he was. There was dancing beginning in another room, and he saw her going towards it. He himself was making his way from acquaintance to acquaintance, towards the card room, when Lord Lynton came up to him.

"Bysshe," he said, "did you know there's a footman looking for you with a message? He asked me if I'd seen you. I said I'd tell you, if I did and thought of it. So now I've told you. Don't be long, we want to start a game."

The Marquis excused himself, and went back into the main

hall, but he saw no one there except a very large footman belonging to the house. The footman, learning who he was, indicated he had put the gentleman with the message in the small salon. He pointed it out to the Marquis, who entered without hesitation. He heard the servant behind him discreetly close the door, even as he saw his error in having underestimated his host.

Facing the door, seated behind his desk, sat the Duke of Salisbury, his face without expression, holding a pistol in one hand directed at his guest, the other hand in repose lightly folded over the mate. Cressy's twin brothers—whom he vaguely remembered—who had been at the rear of the room, one on each side of the door, their swords out, moved one on either side of him.

"If you move or speak," said his Grace with a faint smile at his shocked guest, "I will put two holes through you at once in the places most inconvenient to you." He nodded to the twin at Gore's right, who drew the Marquis' sword out of his belt and deposited it in his own. The Marquis' eyes glinted, but he had no recourse but to stay as he was, waiting.

Still pointing one of his pistols directly at the Marquis, Salisbury spoke in his carefully polite voice: "I shall ask you to say none of these impetuous words that I see hovering on your tongue, but to submit your person to the handling of these gentlemen, my sons." As the Marquis registered no response of any kind, other than his flashing eyes, he continued: "Resist me, if it pleases you—it will come to the same thing in the end. I have servants outside who will come in if I call, but I should prefer we be private."

The Marquis, seeing the force of this observation, suddenly

shrugged, palms out, twisted his lips in a wry smile, and visibly relaxed himself, as at their eccentric will. The extreme courtesy and puzzlement on his face would have given a less sure man than the Duke reason to doubt his cause. But any difficulty in mishandling this urbane peer did not appear to disturb his Grace. He nodded to his sons. One of the twins extracted his own silk handkerchief, and also the Marquis', and with a fair amount of deftness pushed the Marquis' into his startled mouth and bound his own over it and knotted it behind. The sangfroid of what could still be seen of the Marquis' countenance did not appear to alter, for the silk covered the angry flush that rose in his cheeks at this incredible indignity.

The twins indicated with the points of their swords that he should walk forward towards their father at his desk. Kit pulled over a chair with curved flat wooden armpieces and motioned him to it. As he hesitated, the twin behind at his left, whom he recognised as his old acquaintance Timothy, spoke quietly: "Please sit, Bysshe. You must do this, or we must compel you." Again yielding, the Marquis like a cat with elaborate grace picked his way to the front of the little chair, sat down on the seat and leaned back, his eyelids narrowed, looking at neither twin but surveying his host, who reached into a drawer with one hand, and motioning slightly with the pistol, brought out a handful of several lengths of silk cord, the kind used to hold back heavy curtains, which he laid on the desk. They had apparently come from the curtains in the room, which were hanging loose. The twins took them, looking slightly embarrassed, and quickly bound the Marquis' arms to the arms of the chair, which he obligingly rested in position, clearly implying that any indignity was preferable to their touch. The look of shock rose again in his eyes when he realised their intention to fasten each of his legs to a chair leg, but since there was no practical help, he suffered them to break his ease and do as they pleased with his limbs. Their last thought was to loop a cord several times around the back of the chair and his chest, and then at a word from their father, they withdrew from the room through a small side door that gave onto another waiting room, not the main hall.

The Duke looked at his uncomfortable guest without trace of any embarrassment. Indeed, his expression was hard to read at all. His voice was measured and collected, only his eyes menaced. "I must beg leave of you, my lord Gore, for these—contrivings." He waved his hand deprecatingly. "I had the wish to speak to you privately on a subject of a somewhat explosive nature. I have not a great deal of time; my guests will expect my presence. I frankly do not choose to spend it listening to you say what both of us will know to be lies. I *know*, you see, what you have done to my daughter, and I do not need to hear anything you might have to say on that part of our subject." Watching the Marquis and his furious and indignant eyes, he added: "I daresay you think you have a great deal to say; but it does not interest me. Had you the liberty of your limbs and your tongue, we should have a long scene to go through before we arrived at the point we are now at, if we arrived at all."

The Duke paused for a moment, then resumed: "I should like, of course, to kill you. I assume you know that. But that I am not going to do—at least, not yet." Only the slightest tremor in his voice betrayed the emotion he must feel. He continued in his measured voice: "I have called you here to give you the opportunity to ask me for the hand of my daughter in marriage. You will ask it of your own accord, or you will ask it under the persuasion of my two sons and a large mute servant, once a fighter in the Mill, whom I happen to own. I realise the notion may be new to you, and I will give you a few minutes to consider the advantages. While you consider them, let me go further. I shall free your right hand long enough to sign the settlement, which I have here drawn up—and to write a note to your servants in which you will request your clothes to be sent to our country estate where you plan to make a visit of some weeks' stay, in fact, until your marriage to my daughter is—solemnised."

During this speech, the Marquis had felt himself seized by various emotions and thoughts, many of them unfamiliar. The silk handkerchief jammed in his mouth was a singularly novel and unpleasant sensation, and he found himself thinking of the discomforts to which he had so carelessly put Cressida with more imaginative sympathy and something briefly akin to remorse; but the remorse was quickly dissolved in his own indignation. The thought fleetingly touched his mind that it was to make him have such thoughts that he had been put to this discomfort and humiliation—and the quick rage the idea caused him swallowed up his brief bud of compassion, so alien to his nature as almost to have passed unnoticed else. Personal fear, however, did not enter his thoughts, either from courage, or conceit. But he felt a novel respect for this old man that he found surprising. He had underestimated the old fox, and now he was for it. He was not exactly certain if there was anything in his power now that he could do at all, but he had fixed upon certain resolves. Meanwhile, he looked towards his host unwaveringly, studying him.

The older man rose from his chair and came round the

desk, his hands empty. Moving behind the chair in which the Marquis perforce sat, he undid with some difficulty the knot in the handkerchief and relieved the Marquis of the two. Had he had any saliva left, the Marquis would have liked to have spat upon him, but he lacked the wherewithal, and had to content himself with the full contempt of his countenance, free again to view.

"I would like now to hear what you have to say," the old Duke said.

"I think you are mad," said the Marquis with conviction. "And you have ruined my coat and my lace."

"No, my lord, I am not. But I confess I am indeed bewildered to understand why you should seek out my daughter, whom you hardly know and who surely can have not offended you, to visit so showing a humiliation upon. I would not have thought it of you, on my own accord." A mist briefly obscured the Duke's vision.

"Since I don't know what you're talking about," half drawled the Marquis, "you find me at a loss to know, too. What exactly am I supposed to have done to this girl of yours, whom I doubt I could pick out of the ballroom there by sight?" Like a kind of mocking voice he could faintly hear the music to which the guests were dancing.

"My lord, you have ruined her, as you know very well, and as I know too."

"Ruined her? I? That's a laugh."

"You may laugh if you wish, my lord, but in the end we shall still make the accounting."

"I believe you are serious," said the Marquis slowly. "Who has fixed this on me? Your daughter?"

"I question here, not you, Gore," said the Duke sharply.

"On whose word?" the Marquis persisted. "Girls get hysterical, especially the green ones, and sometimes lie." He thought the Duke would strike him, and he braced himself as well as he could, but the moment passed. "Look, I'm sorry if your daughter's spoiled, but I don't want her, I don't want, in fact, to marry anyone at all. But certainly not your daughter, though I won't make a story of it. Now, m'lord, you've had your game with me, I think it's time an end is made of it. I'm growing bored."

"I, too, Lord Gore." The Duke drew up a small table and laid certain documents upon it. "Read through these papers, please, before you sign."

"Sign? No!" The Marquis laughed shortly. "I'm not in the reading humour. My legs have got the cramp."

"Let me beg that you change your mind, to read these papers, my lord, for you will shortly sign them, read or not." At the stormy look on the Marquis' face, he shook his head. "I assure you that you will, for I mean to see that you do."

"How?" questioned the Marquis.

"By no very subtle means. I shall have you beaten, by my man, as you sit there, until you do. Sooner or later you will sign, and for us all, I hope it will be the sooner."

"Good God! I believe you will." The Marquis gave the matter some thought, and having no particular love for lost causes, decided to capitulate before his face resembled a beaten prize fighter's. In much the grand manner, his voice full of mockery, and other emotions, less defined, he said: "Your Grace, I have admired your daughter for some time from my far-off station, and now most humbly beg your Grace's permission to pay to her my addresses, hoping to win both yours and her consent to wed her."

74

His host nodded, and going to the door called in his two sons, who came in somewhat belligerently. "My lord will write. Free his right hand and give him ink and paper." He waited until both were done. "Now first, as I shall direct you, instruct your servants to this effect." The Marquis, listening, in turn nodded, and with some care, inscribed the note and passed it with excess courtesy to his host to read. His Grace then called for sealing wax. "That is your signet ring?" he said, looking hard at it. He signalled one of his sons to take it from the Marquis' finger, and examined it. "Then please imprint it." When that had been done, he said: "You have, I believe, a race on with Lord Lynton?" The Marquis looked surprised, but he again nodded. "You will please withdraw from it." The Marquis inscribed the second note without protest and handed it as before to the Duke. The Duke approved it and the Marquis again impressed it. The Duke then put the ring in a drawer of his desk. If he saw, the Marquis made no comment.

He found his heart beating curiously as he surveyed the longer documents. The first was a simple contract of promise to wed, and that, hardly glancing at it, he signed, his host cosigned, and the sons witnessed. The second, longer document, of settlement and dowry, he looked at cursorily and requested his lawyer dispose of, but this was not allowed.

"You will find it is the usual dowry," said the Duke. "There are no tricks; but her inheritance, you will see, goes direct to her children, or back into our family in the event of her death within the next ten years. In all cases, the income from her trust is to be kept for her children, indefinitely."

"Her children?" queried the Marquis with a lifted eyebrow. "By any parentage or by mine?"

The twin to his left lifted a hand and would have hit him, but his father intervened his stick.

"Not yet, Kit," the Duke said. "The man's tied. And we are talking business matters. It will keep. 'Her children, whosoever by.' Then here, you see, I settle on her these sums for her personal use, we call it 'pocket fare.' It is my intention, my lord Gore, that in this marriage you should neither gain nor lose financially."

The third paper, though short, caused the blood to rise furiously in the Marquis' cheeks, and then subside like a flood, leaving him suddenly pale. Briefly, though precisely in it he, in his name, confessed to the seizure, kidnapping, and carnal rape of the Duke of Salisbury's daughter Cressida on the night of the alleged first of May. For the first time, a note of sincerity entered his voice.

"This paper I do not sign," he said flatly and resolutely, and put down the pen. For answer, only, Salisbury put the pen once again into his hand, and pointed to the place.

The Marquis shook his head firmly. "I will not sign this. It is a lie."

"Call in Bernard, then," his host said, and instructed his eldest son to tie the Marquis' hand once more.

"Wait," the Marquis said with some desperation. The older man eyed him narrowly.

"We have spent already too much time."

"I have signed your damned bloody papers, the Devil knows why," the Marquis said, looking savagely at the twins who together were attempting to resecure his wrist. "I don't, except I like my face as it is, and I daresay I can deal with your daughter as soon as anyone. But I won't go into this business

you seem so set on, acknowledging in my hand any such thing.
You ought not to want me to. Haven't you any pride? I have. I
daresay she's got some. Leave it to her."

"She won't see this paper. Sign, Gore, you haven't got the
choosing."

The Marquis shook his head. "You've made a mistake, and
I'm damned if I'm going to help you out of it. I don't sign
lies."

"Only tell them?" His Grace of Salisbury turned away and
took his older son aside and spoke to him. The Marquis
watched with some apprehension the twin's purposeful exit
through the smaller door. He believed his only hope to salvage
anything at all from this debacle lay in complete disavowal,
but the prospect of his helpless state that he saw ahead alarmed
him. When he spoke again, it was with a coolness that he did
not feel.

"I should have thought you would have minded knocking
up a helpless man."

"My daughter was helpless," murmured the Duke. The
Marquis winced inwardly. "Under the circumstances I do not
mind at all. I am even eager."

"Well, you've got a husband in the offing now for your
damaged goods—" the Marquis paused—"I suppose she really
is?—but if you damage me as well, she might not want me.
Have you taken her opinion? What you have left for her when
you finish might scare her."

The face of the Duke had suffused with anger, but his voice
remained cold. "There are blows, my lord, that wound without
disfiguring."

"Wound away, then. Let your damned mute, or whatever

he is, see my humiliation and your dishonour. But be sure he'll somehow tell it. I must endure you, but you will not make me sign your paper." He shut his eyes, and relaxed back against the chair, for whatever easy minutes still remained to him.

"You do not seem afraid," said the Duke thoughtfully.

"Of course I am afraid," snapped the Marquis. "What do you take me for? Get on with it. I never thought to be a martyr for a silly chit." He shut his eyes again, which was a pity, for he would have been gratified to see the faint gleam of doubt that for a moment wavered in his host's eyes. He did not see his host cross the room, to countermand his order and give a new one. But when nothing continued to occur, after a bit, he opened his eyes, to see his host watching him narrowly.

"Very well—," the Duke said. "I yield this point for the moment—another time we will come back to it again."

"Another time?" said the Marquis faintly. "I had hoped you perceived your error."

"I perceive no such thing, my lord. Your character surprises me—I do not fit it in—but I find no change in the facts as I know them."

"Facts?" murmured the Marquis. "What are these facts?"

"You know them. The unusual part is that I know them, too."

"Indeed. I am devilish uncomfortable in your chair but I would like to be enlightened. If you knew about it, as you keep telling me, why did you let the man go on?" He felt then that he had pressed his host too far. Yet such was his growing despair that he knew a desire to incense his host into some sudden violence, so making an end to the situation entirely, but it immediately occurred to him that it was more a lack of dinner than of any real loss of espoir. He thought his host was aware of his feelings, for he only said, with a downward look:

"Enough of this, my lord. Let us not begin again. You will not provoke me. You need not waste your efforts trying. I am leaving you intact only so that you may consider how you will offer to my daughter. She will shortly be here." He smiled, though not pleasantly.

"Here?" The Marquis' brows lifted. "Like this?"

"How else, considering?" remarked his host. "It will be no stranger than at pistol point, and I daresay she will understand the reasons."

The Marquis was genuinely shocked. "Then gag me, too. You might as well. I'll not speak word."

"I think you will." The Duke gave the matter some thought and offered a compromise: "I can put your cloak around you, and free one hand."

The Marquis gave an exasperated laugh. "Your Grace, undo these silly cords; they have achieved your aims. You may have my word I will not leave your company. But let me meet my future wife upon my feet."

His host shook his head. "Your word is of little value here. And I think you will both find that you have met before."

The Marquis pushed the angry and impatient oaths back that he would have liked to utter. "I think not, sir. But leave it. It is time to speak plainly. It may suit you to have me grovelling and exposed and muttering *mea culpa*'s, but I will *never* do it for you—believe that; and if you want your daugh-

ter's dignity, whatever she's got left, preserved, you'll let me
carry off this business in a more usual manner. I will endorse
to do it, so long as she's about, or we're in public. In private,
I leave myself at your disposal. Totally." The face of the
Duke remained blank and unmoved. "What *can* I give you
more than that? Believe me, I don't want to. But if you embarrass me here and now, in front of her, you will embarrass
her as well—yes, I say *embarrass*—and *nothing* you can do to
me will make me help you then."

His host still hesitated. A faint knock was heard at the
door.

"Good God, man," said the Marquis urgently, "what more
do you require? You have me. I admit that. Now let me
act."

Some faint doubt worked. His host nodded, and bent to the
knots.

"Cut them, man," said the Marquis, "or it will be too late.
You can buy more. I may not be able to stand yet."

"They will wait," said his host, nodding to his younger son
by the door who moved to help. "One moment." His wrists
free, the Marquis rubbed them vigorously, and shook the lace
into place over the red grooves where the cords, tied by the
indignant twins, had dug into his skin.

"What is to prevent your shooting me down, after you have
the ceremony you want?" asked the Marquis curiously, as the
remaining knots were undone.

"Nothing at all," said his host urbanely. "I probably shall,
unless Cressida should grow fond of you."

"Good God!" said the Marquis again. "I never knew
you."

"You should have done so," answered the Duke quietly. "If I minded your taking my horse, what was that to your taking my daughter?" He moved a little away and turned his back on the Marquis.

VII

THE REMEETING

Released at last, the Marquis pulled his legs into a more normal angle, and stood up stiffly, and adjusted his coat. One cord was twisted about his stocking and he handed it to his host politely, saying: "Your property, I think?" It had only been for a few minutes that he had lost possession of himself at all, and now his old manner fell upon him. He stood negligently at ease by the desk, surveying a lacquered box upon it, his back to the door. He heard it open, but he did not turn at once. When he did, he found Cressy's two brothers had left the room, and only Cressy and her father remained. He bowed, and briefly raised her fingers to his lips.

He himself surveyed her curiously, for although he must have seen her briefly at balls and galas, since she grew up, he had paid her no attention, and their last meeting had been in darkness and subdued light. He rather liked what he saw. He also saw at once, to his satisfaction, that she had no recognition of him at all. Her hand did not tremble in his, and her voice was firm, though wondering.

"My father told me that you had something to say to me?" He met her clear gaze with difficulty, believing that with his first words she might know him.

"You know me?" he asked hesitantly. He thought she must hear the furious beating of his heart, but his face showed none of his emotion, for if she knew him he would have no hope at all.

She smiled gracefully and inclined her head. "I have been told your name, my lord, but not your business."

He flushed slightly, then smiled at her engagingly. "Miss Daviot, please do not regard it as an impertinence, since we have hardly met, but I have asked your father if I might pay my addresses to you." A startled look came into her eyes, and she blushed deeply, and the smile left her face entirely.

"But I do not wish—" she said in confusion. She turned her head suddenly to look towards her father who had removed himself a little way and was standing by the mantle, examining its design.

"What do you not wish, Miss Daviot?" the Marquis asked courteously.

"I do not understand!" she cried, and then she said: "I do not even know you!—Is this your wish or my father's?"

"It is my wish, Miss Daviot, but I believe I have your father's approval, if you will give me yours." She looked disturbed and unhappy, and for a moment his heart was moved for her.

"White becomes you, Miss Daviot," he said, bowing again. At her deeper flush, he realised the tactlessness of his remark, but he passed over it. "I remarked you across the floor."

"I did not see you," she said in a low, embarrassed voice, bluntly.

The gallantry he would have spoken died on his lips, as he recollected that having once seen her, he had taken care she should not see him. That time seemed a long time ago to him now. But since she had been standing by a mirror, he must have been in her view. He thought she must have seen him, and he was somehow piqued to have been unnoticed. Since she would not or could not speak, he collected himself towards a further effort.

"Your father has invited me to come down to Rotherby for a visit of a fortnight or some weeks, and it is my hope there to further our acquaintance."

She replied in a low voice: "I shall be happy to see a friend of my father, and I hope your stay will be an enjoyable one, but please, though I do not want to give offence to you, it is not my wish to marry anyone at all."

He was surprised, and he looked at her more searchingly. "Your father has not spoken of this subject to you, I see? I am sorry to have distressed you."

She shook her head, her eyes lowered. He was at a loss to understand the particular nature of her shyness or of her distress which was clearly real. She seemed to be giving very little of her attention to him, and his dress and manner were so changed, he was ready to take oath that she did not connect his present self with his previous one. In fact, her distress did not have that quality. It had rather a different nature—with a shock that actually shook him, he realised that she had not told her father of her adventure, and that her embarrassment sprang from what she believed to be her private knowledge of her state. It was then as he had first thought, in his confidence, so long ago on that evening. But the rightness of his surmise no longer gratified him. He could have laughed aloud, thinking of the melodramatic capers of the evening, and his victim sublimely unconscious of them all. But another look at her quenched the wish, standing there ironically in her white dress, the colour flushing her cheeks, her eyes lowered, and somehow, it occurred to him, very brave. Why had she not? His thoughts shifted and he forgot her. How, then, had Salisbury known? Someone else had told him. Who? A servant? Unlikely. A member of the Club? Improbable, yet it seemed the only possibility. Who then? And why? And how? The name had not been told. He had not time to think it out, but he reflected grimly that when he shed this coil, as he believed some way no doubt he should, he had a reckoning to make. He abruptly put his thoughts aside, realising the silence was lengthening.

"Perhaps," he said, "when you have had time to consider, you will let me speak to you further."

"On any subject you like," she said with a shy smile, "please, but this." He thought of the signed contract, and her father's plans, and wondered what he would make of her reluctance. In point of fact, he did not know what to make of it himself, for it seemed to him to be what she should of all things most welcome. She showed no shrinking. Was she standing out because of some feeling of honour? His mood, of brief interest, suddenly changed to irritation, which he tried not to show, and offering her his arm, he took her to her father where he stood waiting, a few steps away.

"The lady likes not my suit," he said flatly. He felt tired and full of anticlimax, until he saw the menace in her father's eyes.

"How is this? You have frightened her?"

"No, sir," she said with soft respect, "indeed he has not, but I do not aspire to be his wife. It is an honour I appreciate, but I do not wish it." The Marquis heard her with feelings of brief gratitude.

"And if I say you shall?"

She lifted half-frightened eyes. "Then I will beg you not to urge me now. The contract is too sudden—I must think." Her voice faltered. "I hardly know this man, except by name. I had not thought of marriage; it is not in my mind."

"No?" His voice was incredulous. "Then put it there."

"I pray your Grace to be not angry with me, but give me yet a little time." She smiled at him winningly: "You have never come the tyrant over me before, sir. I hardly know you in this new role."

His face softened and he took her hand: "Well, go, then, Cressy, with your brothers back to the room and excuse me to my guests. We must talk again, you and I, at another time— meantime, I will speak with the Lord Gore. I had thought the prospect of a marriage with my lord to have affected you much otherwise than this."

The men bowed to her, and she made a small curtsy and went out on the arm of her brother Kit. After they had gone, the two men stood in brief silence, the unspoken words burning the air between them. The Marquis spoke first. He said flatly: "You have made a mistake, how I cannot imagine and you will not tell me, but I am content to overlook it. I will go now."

The Duke lifted his hooded eyes, and at the look in them even the Marquis flinched. "I do not mistake. Hold your peace," he said in a voice of command. "You do not leave this room without my permission, and I think I have not given you that."

The Marquis flushed. "You cannot be serious. Your girl don't know me. And she don't look ruined to me," he added. "I consider our agreement dissolved. I won't be a scapegoat to your whim. I am leaving now."

"You would be advised to stay," said the Duke meaningfully.

"Advice be damned," said the Marquis, and turned on his heel, but it was a foolish gesture. The Duke picked up a silver whistle he had lying on his desk and blew on it. Kittredge and Timothy, returned from escorting their sister, opened the small door and surged in, and the muscular footman stepped inside the larger double doors, locking both behind him. The Marquis, well-accustomed to working out and too angry to regard his new coat, refused the offices of reason. For several breathless moments he stood his Grace's reinforcements off, but their strength in numbers and weight prevailed over his fury. Nevertheless, he raged on, cursing the Duke and giving his opinion of him in expert obscenity, until the coldly brutal handling of the footman possessed of the boxer's skill exhausted him. He stood panting, in the grasp of the three of them, his mouth bleeding, his wrists now bound behind his back with the same type of silk cord as before. The Duke had not moved from where he stood.

"You amuse me, Gore," his lordship said coldly. "I am happy you afforded me an excuse for this pleasure. Shall we have it again, or will you be quiet now and believe that I mean what I say?" Bearing his handkerchief in his hand, he walked up purposefully over to the Marquis, who stiffened.

"God's teeth, no!" exclaimed the Marquis in horror. "I am quiet now!"

The Duke paid not the slightest attention to the Marquis' words. Carefully, with considerable grace, he wiped the signs of combat away from the Marquis' mouth, and then discarded his handkerchief to his footman. The Marquis this time wisely held his peace, and waited for the Duke to address him, which after a time he did. He signalled his sons and his retainer to release their grasp on the Marquis' arms, and said, tentatively: "I do not consider the assurance which you gave me dissolved by this rash testing of my purposes."

"What conceivable difference can it make to you now?" the Marquis asked without great interest.

"Let it suffice that it does make one. I do not release you from it."

"Take my word then, take anything you like," snapped the Marquis savagely.

"I hold you to that," the Duke said urbanely, bowing. The Marquis, overcome by the dangerous absurdity of his position, threw back his head and uttered a short, sharp laugh of unamused exasperation.

His host said abruptly, "I shall take you down myself tonight." He gave rapid instructions for the journey to Bernard and sent the footman out to make the preparations and ready the chaise. But on second thoughts, he changed the instructions for daybreak in the morning, and sent a servant on ahead by horseback to forewarn his establishment. He ordered the Marquis to drink a light sleeping potion, and ruthlessly enforced the order. He then sent the Marquis upstairs with Timothy and Kittredge, promising to make his adieus and excuses, and himself went back to his guests.

The Marquis, his travelling cloak thrown about his shoulders, preceded the younger twin up the stairs. He had reminded Timothy that he had given a version of his word, but Timothy had preferred not to accept it, pointing out that his father would give it to him, as he put it, if the Marquis decided suddenly again to go off his word.

"I'm deuced sorry about it, Bysshe," he said, "but it is your own fault, you know."

On their way to the stairs, they met only the old Duke of Renton in the hall, near the door, to whom they bowed and passed compliments.

"You're looking a bit knocked up," the old Duke said. "You ought to get more sleep. You young men keep bad hours, worse than we did." He offered his snuff to the Marquis, who smiled and thanked him but declined because his hands were tied. The Duke guffawed at the witticism, and took himself off, but Timothy gave the Marquis a severe warning on such levity. The Marquis, feeling light-headed, only smiled again.

Timothy had been told to take their guest with him to his own room and to make him both secure and comfortable. His ideas on this were not complicated. After giving the Marquis opportunity to attend to his needs, he left him in his clothes on the chaise longue, a wrist knotted to each of its arms, and a kind of loose leash looped about his neck which Timothy attached to his own wrist.

"If you need anything in the night," he said, "just pull."

"I don't see why you bother," said the Marquis. "The girl don't even want me."

"I wouldn't worry about *that*," said Timothy, putting on his nightshirt and curling comfortably down into his soft bed. "She'll come round. You did." And settled himself to sleep. The Marquis followed soon after. His mind was not accustomed to introspection, and the complications of the night defied his analysis. It seemed a little thing, after so much yielding, to yield to slumber.

VIII

THE EXCHANGE

The journey down to the country seat of Lord Salisbury was accomplished in various stages. The Duke woke the slumbering younger men before the light had fully broken. The Marquis' servants had not yet sent over his portmanteau and his shaving kit, and the Duke's man Bernard proceeded to shave him with Timothy's equipment, while Timothy pulled his clothes on. The Marquis breakfasted alone on rolls and butter in Bernard's company on the chaise longue, while Timothy went down to breakfast on ham with his father. Torn between two places that needed him at one time, the Duke sent the Marquis in the first coach with both Timothy and Kit, and Bernard to ride on top. The twins were to take turns riding, the voluble Timothy taking the first turn by horse, and the grimmer Kit sitting morosely in the carriage with the Marquis in the grey light of the dawn.

The Marquis never remembered so unpleasant a journey, being more accustomed to riding out than to sitting in. His feet had been hobbled as some sort of precaution, though he had the partial use of his hands to help with the swaying of the coach, and across from him Kit sat glumly with a pistol at the cock. "That thing will go off, you know, when we hit a bump," he had said, to no effect—so he leaned back into one corner of the upholstery and shut his eyes and pretended to sleep. Hours and hours later, it seemed, after various stops and embarrassments and unsavoury refreshments, they reached Rotherby. Kit had been told which room to give their guest, and had escorted him there and left the giant Bernard to keep him company. But since the windows were high and small and casemented in his room, the footman's presence seemed unneeded. But when the Marquis suggested he go out and lock the door behind him, he only received a grunt in answer. So he gave himself up to boredom and to surveying his surroundings.

There was not much to see. Through the window he could see the tips of trees with the bright new green of May. The room had been newly done in blue and white, with a pleasant luxuriousness in the quality of the rugs and furnishings, except for an old-fashioned velvet prie-dieu in one corner. However, it had a familiar air. From the windows and the position and various undisguisable signs of age and use he suspected it of having been an old nursery. With a shock he recognised it as having been the room he had stayed in, that Christmas holiday how many years ago, he scarcely could remember them. He did not believe he had been placed there by accident. The memory his host showed himself to possess frightened him for a moment, but he shook the feeling off. If his Grace wished him to think such thoughts, he would not oblige him. It was just a room, and perhaps not after all the same. There might be several such exactly like it on that side of the house. He prowled round three times inquisitively, and then settled down to wait.

The Duke started out some three hours later in his personal travelling chaise and took his daughter in it with him. He had not seen her since the night before, when she had been so strangely formal, and he noticed that she looked even more worn. She made him a curtsy in greeting and kissed his hand, but her lips bore no trace of any smile, and her eyes remained downcast. She would have taken the seat opposite him, but at his prompting she sat beside him, her fingers nervously pleating a fold of her dress. He said nothing out of the ordinary way until the coach had moved onto the road, then he put his hand over her fingers, holding them quiet, and with his other hand, tilted her face up until he could see her desperate eyes, and smiled into them with concern. In the light of her reticence, he hardly knew what to say or how to begin.

Cressy herself solved his problem, saying in a low voice: "I am sorry to have displeased you, sir, last night."

He smiled. "I had thought this marriage would have pleased you. It seemed to me most suitable."

She turned her troubled eyes upon him. "Oh, sir, indeed I am not the wife for his lordship." Her lips trembled, and he thought she might cry, but she did not.

"Why not?" he asked. "There is another man you prefer?"

"No, oh no!" she said. "It is only that I do not think to marry at all."

"Come, Cressy, that's a foolish, missish thing to say. You've kept house for me quite long enough, and now I think you need one of your own. I have been remiss in this." He studied her carefully. "Cannot you like this man?" he asked. "He has a noble house; in time he will be Adversane himself."

"I observed him from a distance at our rout for some time, for he drew attention, though I would not give him so much satisfaction as to tell him so." She smiled slightly. "Just for himself, he is a courteous man, and very well-looking, though somewhat wild, I've heard. I think he is perhaps too gay for me; at heart I am a tame sort of bird. You know that yourself, sir. But I do not think at all whether I like or cannot like." She paused. "The problem does not lie there."

"Where, then?" he asked. She was silent, looking at her lap.

"And if I say, Cressy, that wild or tame, noble or not, well-favoured in your eyes or not, that I do wish for you to listen favourably to this gentleman's suit, what then?"

"Do you compel me, sir?"

"No, Cressy, I have never compelled you to anything, I do not mean to start now; but I am saddened that I lack your confidence. Had your mother lived, she would know better than I what needed to be said." Some tears slid from her eyes, but she did not wipe them away, not wishing to draw attention to them. One fell on his hand which still held hers.

"I would give you my confidence, sir, but I cannot find the words to tell you. If my lord Gore marries me, he could find reason to be disappointed and angry with the match, and me, and you. I could not bear it, sir." She began to sob in earnest. "Please, do not make me."

"Hush, child, hush!" he said, upset by her tears. "I know what you don't wish to tell me. I have known since yesterday."

"You *know?*" Her face was filled with consternation and dismay. "How could you?"

"I have my ways," he said, without explaining. "But I do know, in part, at least." He reached up with a familiar gesture and touched the blunt ends which he had found in her hair the day before, looking at her significantly. She said nothing at all for several minutes, while he sat quietly waiting, watching closely the play of emotions across her face.

"You knew," she said finally, half-bewildered, half-incredulous, "and yet you wanted me to marry with this lord?"

"I know, Cressy, and I do. I think it wise you marry, child, and soon, as soon as it may be. And this noble lord, this Marquis of Gore, is most suitable, being the very man, as I think you would know, who tumbled you into this plight. I make my meaning clear?" He watched the shock cross her face as his meaning penetrated—shock give way to anger and dismay and bewilderment, and then finally amazement, now this emotion, now that, but not disbelief.

"The Marquis of Gore? Why? Why he? Surely you are mistaken!"

"She thinks so too," he remarked to himself grimly, "but she is choosing to play some game with me. I wonder why?"

She in turn read her fate in his relentless face, and her voice faltered piteously: "How do you know? Could you not be mistaken?"

"I am not mistaken. He has boasted of the fact, and shown your lock of hair. But I wondered last night that you yourself did not know. It did not occur to you? You do not seem surprised."

"No. No," she whispered. "I never saw his face." Suddenly she was overcome by indignation. "I do not understand you! You knew, why, even last night you knew, and yet you let such a man come into your house and mock me?" Her eyes flashed with furious humiliation.

"He did not make a mock of you, Cressy, he came to make a reparation."

"Why?" she asked simply.

"Why, for all the obvious reasons, Cressy, I suppose, remorse, regret, that sort of thing—" she shook her head, for he had not seemed remorseful but highly self-possessed—"but principally because I insisted upon it."

"Does he himself say so?"

"No, my dear, I cannot say he does, though he will come to it, in time, I think. But we are both agreed upon this contract, if you will agree, too."

She shook her head in despair. "If it is really so, what is to become of me when I am always with him and totally in his power and at his mercy—for he has none. Oh, sir, I do not know—I am not convinced that this man—my lord Gore—is the man who—" she broke off and continued even more disconnectedly—"I hardly saw him then, the night was dark, his voice and manner were not—were not the same—at least, I think—oh, I cannot like it, sir; I am afraid."

"He will not dare to hurt you, Cressy. You do not need to be afraid. He has a noble name, he will uphold it."

She shook her head, unconvinced still. "I think it cannot be this man. Why would he come then, to our house? Why did he change so suddenly? Either way, I do not see why he should ask to marry me."

"He asked because I insisted," the Duke said dryly.

"Does he then know *you* know?"

"He does indeed," he said more dryly still.

Her hands flew to her cheeks, as if to cool them and to hide their colour. She exclaimed, unbelievingly: "And he is coming to our country house? Oh, sir, I shall be *so* embarrassed. I am sorry you have told me, sir. I thought my unhappiness complete, until now. I do not understand how you permit it, or how he agrees."

"We thought it for the best, and for your good," the Duke said briefly.

She sat in silence, digesting these disagreeable news. Men seemed to her incomprehensible, but she did not say so. She had thought her situation could not be worse, but now it seemed to be.

"Can I say *no*?" she asked.

"You can."

"You will not force me?"

"No, my dear." If he was disappointed, he did not show his disappointment. "But I would like you to have thought his offer over for some few days, most carefully, before you do say *no*."

"If I say *no*, what will you do?"

"I'll send you to the sisters, at Maryhill, at least for a while."

"I should not mind that. It sounds restful." She was silent, thinking. "Would you call my lord Gore out?

"No."

"I'm glad. I should not wish that. I should be afraid for you."

"Afraid for me?" He laughed. "Don't be."

Something in his voice alarmed her. "But I think you do mean to injure him. Oh, sir, I do not wish it. Do not stir yourself."

"That, my dear, will be for my affair," he answered shortly. "But I'd think you'd wish it. The man has injured you. I mean to see he recompenses for the injury, one way or the other. Don't concern yourself about it—he did not about you."

"I think you don't leave me very much choice, sir," she said sadly.

"No more did he!" the Duke said fiercely. Then he added, more gently: "I don't think there *is* much choice, Cressy. I have by good chance found a way to give your honour back to you, and I think we should all be very grateful for it. But if you'd rather not, I must restore your honour in another way. There is no more to it. Now shall we talk of something else? Or would you rather tell me more about it?"

She shook her head, and smiled faintly. "Let's talk of other things."

Not seeing the Marquis or his chaise when they arrived, she assumed he had not yet driven down and was grateful for his absence. She was weary, and retired to her room immediately after a light supper; and since she saw no satisfactory way out of her troubles, she put them out of her mind for the time and went to sleep. Had the decision affected her alone, she would have had no quandary, but her action seemed closely bound with the future of the Marquis, whether she willed it or no.

The Exchange

As for that young man, he saw no one all the day, only the servant Bernard who brought him his meals and silently attended on him, and once the brother Kit who saturninely informed him that his father the Duke would wait upon the Marquis in the morning.

IX

THE DISCIPLINING

The morning dawned fair and fresh, one of those loveliest of mornings in May. The scent of flowering lilac filled the air even inside the Marquis' room and drew him to the narrow windows. Cressy went for a ride after breakfast. The Marquis saw her go, with her brother Timothy, wistfully, out of sight into the green wood. He paced round and round the room, cramped and longing for exercise. He did not look forward to the visit of the Duke, and yet anything seemed preferable to his solitude, which he was not used to, or the company of the silent Bernard. Shortly he wished for his solitude back. He heard the lock turn, and thought it his breakfast, but it was Kit who entered, with the omnipresent Bernard, and curtly ordered him to kneel at the prie-dieu.

"I'm no Priest-lover!" he protested, at which Kit drew his pistol.

"Oh, good lord!" he said, "I'm embarrassed. What's this for?
My so-called sins? You're too damned peculiar in this house,
too serious." He gave an indignant exclamation. "You, take
your damned hands off my shirt! Oh, very well, very well, take
my breeches too, then, if you want them, and we'll all play
games together! Is this how you take the linens in this house?
My neckcloth's soiled."

But Bernard only took his shirt, without the shadow of a
smile, and gripped his hands and fastened them with a strap
on the other side of the stem of the prie-dieu. The Marquis,
blaspheming, began *Pater noster quisquis*—whereupon Kit
turned on his heel and strode out, taking Bernard with him
The Marquis heard the key turn, and then he was left in the
silence which lengthened out uncomfortably. The minutes slid
by, and no one came, and nothing happened.

After a longer while, he heard the lock turn again, and
someone enter, he could not see who, and walk up behind
him. He waited, saying nothing, nor did his visitor speak.
Without warning, he felt a sharp stinging on his shoulders. He
twisted his head round. "Good morning, my lord Duke. I
should have known!"

"Good morning, Gore," returned the Duke, applying his
riding whip again, to good effect. The Marquis gasped and
said nothing more, because the blows were laid on more
strongly, and took his breath away; nor did the Duke because
he was using his breath laying them on. The Marquis did not
know how many strokes he received, or how long a time they
took, but he had come to the point of thinking that if what his
host was waiting for was for him to groan loudly, he would
oblige him, when the whip was laid down.

"A present," said the Duke, breathing hard, "from your father, were he here to give it, and from my daughter's father, with my compliments!"

"My thanks," said the Marquis, between his teeth. "Please do not put yourself to trouble."

"It is my pleasure," said his host sincerely. He walked around to the front and surveyed the Marquis. "You look done in."

"I have not breakfasted," replied the Marquis.

"I will send up a remedy for that shortly," said his host. "Will you sign my paper?"

"What bloody paper?" spat the Marquis.

The Duke pulled it from his inner pocket and unfolded it.

"Oh, God, that?" said the Marquis. "Again? No, I won't."

"Expect me then tomorrow," said his host. He took a small jar he had brought, and began to rub a cold, rather soothing ointment on the inflamed skin of the Marquis' back and shoulders.

"To enable you," he explained, "to get your coat on. Do you think you can?"

"Of course I can. I could at Eton, and they were much worse."

The Duke smiled. "I need practice, I see. I will leave you for a while to think things over, and then Bernard will assist you in your toilet for the afternoon. Your clothes have arrived. You are expected for lunch; luncheon is at two today. We have several other guests." He ignored the Marquis' look of surprise. "Mix with them as you please, but use discretion. You may walk with Cressy if in company on the grounds; you may not ride. I expect you to be in eyesight of Kittredge or Timothy or myself at all times when you are out of this room. No tête-à-têtes with anyone, of course. I hold you to your word, despite your lapse. You do remember?"

"I recollect it well," the Marquis said. "You have certainly taken me at it."

His host bowed, and withdrew, leaving the Marquis to his penitence. He had been his own master for so many years that he had forgotten until now a trick that he had learned as a small boy of disassociating himself from an unbearable present. Now, for the first time in many years feeling the power, not merciless but relentless, of another person, the old escape came to his aid and he took it gratefully. Unaccustomed emotions were near him, and foreign thoughts, and it was these as much as discomfort that he wished to evade. Entering half an hour later, with coffee and rolls, Bernard found him motionless, almost seemingly asleep, although his eyes were open. He had nothing to say as the mute released his wrists, except to ask him to help him up. The big man, for all his brute seeming, was a skilful valet, and between the two of them, and his portmanteau that the mute brought up, he began to feel more himself again. His shoulders were stiff, but not impossibly. He went down to meet the company.

One of the guests was an old friend of his from school, now a friend of Kit's, whom he had not seen for several years, for he had moved to the North. Two others he knew by sight, a middle-aged country gentleman and his wife from Sussex, his host's age, and their son and daughter whom he did not know. He sighed, and set himself to charm. He knew how to act, none better, when he chose, and now he did choose. His reputation and even his survival lay on the chance, but his breeding made the play effortless.

As for Cressy, his heart had wholly hardened towards her, at sometime during that morning, and he no longer cared what her sufferings might be. His part was the simple one of himself come to woo her, and this he proceeded to do, gracefully and skilfully, without self-consciousness, since his feelings were unengaged. It was a game he played, no more, but he enjoyed the barely concealed surprise on the faces of his host and his sons. He noted, however, a change in Cressy's manner since the last time he saw her, only two nights before. Her responses were the proper ones, but a shadow lay on her face, and sometimes he surprised her looking closely at him, or listening with a special attentiveness. He knew then that her father had enlightened her, of how much he hardly wished to try to guess, and that she had not entirely believed him. But her reluctance to entertain his suit was gone. He did not wonder why. He did her the injustice of believing she was simply and practically glad to have her difficulties so resolved.

For himself, he resolved to perplex her, if he could, and fan her little doubts into larger ones. He took her walking in the arbour, fetching her shawl with the customary gallantries, and the ache beneath his coat served as a spur. In this he was successful. She found it impossible to believe that the two men could be the same, although she found it nearly as hard to doubt her father, or her own perceptions. Forgetting the performance she herself was putting on, she could not believe anyone so urbane, so civil, so aloof, had ever lain with her in the most impassioned intimacy. Her thoughts made her flush, and he looked down at her, his eyes dancing as he wickedly read her thoughts and rejoiced. Accustomed to intimacies, the memory shook him not at all, but he enjoyed her confusion, and played upon it, in the manner of a gallant, teasing her.

"Why, Miss Daviot," he quizzed, "you blush. I vow you've turned less cold to me than I dared hope."

"Perhaps, my lord," she said with a slight smile. "I think you should take me in now. I see my father waiting, and he looks impatient."

"Let us walk in the rose garden, Miss Daviot, tomorrow," he suggested.

"But the roses do not bloom until June. It is quite bare there now, they have hardly come in bud."

"Until June?" he said musingly, his thoughts suddenly caught. "I wonder if I must be here then?"

"Must?" she retorted, looking at him quizzingly in her turn. "Must, Lord Gore? Then I tax you, leave now!" He looked at her suspiciously, but he could find no mockery in her face.

"My heart compels me here: I must indeed stay!" he said extravagantly, and surprised a look of amusement in her eyes at his atrociously transparent lie. Angered, he took her fingers in his, and with audible passion, though not the tender passion of love, in his voice, he said seriously, bending his eyes on hers with meaning: "I do not jest. I must stay here—until you or the roses bloom for me."

He had his revenge. The colour rose in her cheeks, she dropped her eyes, and attempted to disengage her fingers from his. But he held them in his, and tucked one small hand under his arm. They made a pretty picture to the observers nearer the house. If she recognised the steely strength of those fingers, and had misgivings about the part she played, she made no sign, but walked beside him demurely, in silence. He did not press her further. But she thought to herself: "He knows what my father thinks of him. If he is innocent, he is a very good man (though they say in town he has a somewhat dangerous reputation); if he is not, he is a fiend, and I should guard myself. Either way, I shall enjoy this," she resolved, "for he is enjoying it." She raised her face to his with her bewitching smile flooding eyes and lips, which he had not seen (and not many had, since her mother's death), and enjoyed his sudden discomfiture, as he had enjoyed hers. But privately, she wondered how they could either one continue in this vein.

She was mistaken. Each with relief had found the other capable of both playing and sustaining what for some might be an impossible part. They settled down, like an unexcited engaged couple of long standing, into a comfortable routine of dances, calls, rides, formal dinners, routs. Their hearts unengaged, each watched the other to falter, and enjoyed the game for the skill of it, not the game itself. She never caught him out again. Essentially aloof, he made an amusing companion. She was more transparent in her waverings of opinion, but then he had the advantage over her in exact knowledge of the case. They both enjoyed the bafflement of her protecting men. Sometimes, even, the twins seemed to forget, but he knew her father never did.

Every morning, so regularly he needed no clock, Bernard came, alone now. The Marquis knew so well the outcome he made no more demur, but bent his knees and allowed his hands to be bound. His host entered, sometimes quickly, sometimes delayed, and dispassionately flogged him, offered him the paper to sign, annointed his shoulders, and briefed him on the day ahead. Sometimes, improbably, they even talked together. The Marquis spoke to him as he might have spoken to himself—he had gone beyond anger—and the Duke replied in like vein. It was a bond that did not exist outside the one situation. The Duke, perhaps mistakenly, believed that only if the Marquis could be brought to admit his fault and the justice of the Duke's treatment of him, could the marriage he was forcing upon both the man and his daughter have any chance of success. The Marquis, for his part, was determined on the course he had originally taken of maintaining a complete innocence and ignorance and keeping his inner privacy intact. He felt otherwise he could not himself survive. Within the circle of their opposing aims and determinations, they met not only as evenly matched opponents, despite the Duke's advantage, but curiously and reluctantly, almost as friends. The Duke laid on the punishment he thought necessary for his purpose, impersonally. The Marquis received it, if not impersonally, with patience and a kind of respect. It became something they went through, testing each the other's continuing strength and resolve. Then they passed on to the other events of the day, as if the morning had not been.

The Marquis seemed to live in two worlds. The purity of his nights and the sobriety of his present life, compensated for the strain and the mistreatment, and at first he felt very well, better than he had for several months. He began to wonder how long it had been since he had been so sober, to think that he must have been half-drunk for years, without knowing it. In some ways he felt he was making a retreat, a purification, with fastings, penances, soul-searching, meditations, or at least, empty stretches of time; he even did some reading, and observed the management of the country estate with an interest before unknown to him. He found himself waking early, clear-headed and clear-eyed, as he had when a young boy. Like Cinderella, he was instructed to withdraw early in the evenings, and one of the twins always found excuse, if he forgot, to see that he did; but until then, in the afternoons and evenings, his life, though temperate, was much as it had always been. Had he been a thinking man, it might have bothered him, but he was accustomed to living in the present moment, and he shifted without difficulty between the two worlds, helped by the fact that they were secret and disconnected, except for his host's knowledge.

So matters continued for a fortnight, the only change for the Marquis being in a loss of the well-being of the first week, and a growing dread of the daily disciplining; and so they would have continued, for Cressy herself desired no change, except for a chance mistake. Cressy, sent to a room nearby, mistook the room, and opened the Marquis' door, which Bernard had by chance left unlocked. The Marquis had fainted, and Bernard had thrown a cloak about him for warmth and gone to fetch the Duke again in a great hurry. Seeing the Marquis on his knees, she thought he was at prayer, and quietly withdrew. He did not turn his head and did not know. But she was somehow puzzled, for prayer and the Marquis did not seem in keeping.

That night, she said: "How is it, my lord, I never see you until noon? Must you always sleep so late?"

The Marquis laughed shortly; his host, his patience worn thin, had afforded him an unusually hard morning. "I generally find myself occupied until then," he said.

She had no encouragement, but she continued, hesitatingly: "I came by chance upon you at your prayers this morning, but you did not see me."

"Oh? I did not know. Your father helps me at them."

"Helps you?"

"Assists. Ask him yourself."

"Does—does he persist in urging you—?" she faltered.

"Lord, Miss Daviot, how is it you think I'm here? Take it any way you like, but it is not by my own will, I do assure you." He spoke roughly, and she had a sudden glimpse in his eyes of the cruelty of which he was capable.

He saw the little edifice they had built crash down. Her face grew quite white, and he thought she would faint, but even as he offered to fetch her some restorative, she rallied herself, smiled wanly, and made a trivial excuse.

"You are not feeling well, I think," she said, excusing him, too. Hiding her speculations under lowered eyelids, she dropped her handkerchief suddenly, and looked down at it expectantly.

He grimaced and said, "I cannot stoop, my dear. I've strained myself with exercises."

"It is no matter," she said, her tacit question answered, "—a piece of cloth—" She looked at him squarely. "I am not entirely a fool, my lord. I cannot stop this marriage if I would."

"Cannot you?" he asked, disbelievingly. For a brief second his hidden self looked out at her from his eyes, tormented and desperate.

She shook her head and did not explain.

"Then let us do it quickly," he said, "for I cannot take much more."

She did not ask for explanation. "I will speak to my father," she answered.

The next morning she passed by the Marquis' room again, and stayed, listening, until her father came out. He was shocked and angered to see her, but he said no word until they had reached her own room. She asked him to come in, but she made no reference to the Marquis, and he thought she had heard nothing, or had not understood. She came quickly to the point.

"I have accepted your plans, and I would like the marriage to take place as soon as possible, sir," she informed him.

"And the Marquis?"

"It is his wish, too."

"The betrothal is announced already in London," he informed her in his turn. She looked surprised. "We will announce it here tonight; then we will take a trip to France and wed you quietly there. Can you be ready in a week?" He looked embarrassed. "Have you found reason for haste?"

"I can be ready," she answered quietly. "I am only weary of this strain." She put her hand on his arm. "Let us leave tomorrow. I can fix a dress as easily in Paris as here."

The Duke of Salisbury, his face sad but stern, kissed his daughter and agreed.

X

THE WEDDING

So it was done. They left the next morning for the Channel
crossing, the Marquis, Cressy, her father, her twin brothers,
and the ever present Bernard. They travelled in two chaises,
the bridegroom carefully escorted by the brothers of the bride.
Cressy did not see the Marquis again from the time of their
last meeting before she spoke with her father until she saw
him standing at their wedding. The Duke was careful she
should not. The Marquis had been taken into a cabin on
board the Duke's yacht before the Duke and Cressy's chaise
arrived, and he was removed from it after their chaise had
started on the second stage of the journey. He had been
thoughtful and quiet and had given his escorts no trouble,
and no argument, letting them do as they liked with his person, for he saw from their set faces that they would not listen

to him. When they reached Paris, they put up at two hotels, not informing their friends of their arrival, for the several days while the Duke made the arrangements necessary for so sudden and hurried a marriage. During that time Cressy wondered at the Marquis' continued absence but she knew he did not love her or wish to be with her; and she had her own arrangements to make which, though not extensive, involved her time.

The Marquis did not go out at all. Bernard or one of the twins stayed with him at all times, and he was not permitted to leave his room. He gave no thought to escaping from his immediate situation. The Duke's ruthless intention he knew too well, and he was only relieved that the Duke was situated with his daughter in a different hotel than his. He wished his host to take no more interest in him. His initial interest had been to have the Marquis placed in the smaller inner room of the apartments, where the hotel servants did not come; and he had caused light fetters to be put on the Marquis' ankles, and his wrists as well. The Marquis had been inwardly indignant, since leaving had not been in his mind, but he had not wasted his strength resisting them.

"I am not a studhorse to hobble," he protested only the once. "I said I would come."

"I believe you, but I cannot afford to lose you; you can surely see that," was the only reply the Duke gave him, before he left him.

So he sat by the window, his proud beautiful face unsmiling, as stern and haughty as his host's, and watched the people pass on the wide streets far below him, and the chaises and the carts come and go, and waited for his nuptials.

They were married not in the Chapel de le Saint Esprit but

by a Protestant clergyman in the Embassy. The Marquis looked elegant, pale, and resolved, but they did not know on what he had resolved. Cressy looked tired and pale and subdued, no radiant bride at all. She had not had a new dress made, but had used the white dress she had worn the night the Marquis began his suit. She spoke her vows in a small voice, not looking at anyone, and the Marquis, far from pitying her, found himself hating her. It was bad to be married, and unwillingly, but intolerable to a little mouse who looked so sad and ill. Ill? The thought now made him blanch, but he thought, "Surely not!"

The unjoyous ceremony having somehow come to an end, the wedding party made ready to cross the street to where the larger of the two chaises stood. Cressy had been handed by her husband into the coach where she sat quietly, with no more expression than he on her face. Her father had not kissed her, for it was not his intention to leave her. The Marquis, about to make the step up to sit beside her, stood with Bernard by the door. The Duke and his sons had not crossed, but they were speaking to friends at the Embassy. The Duke, his aim achieved, was less vigilant; his back was slightly turned to catch a remark of Kit's about the wedding breakfast that was to follow. The horses began to show signs of impatience, and Bernard was climbing onto the box. Unexpectedly another chaise came lurching down the street. The Marquis, waiting for such a moment, took it swiftly. He swung himself lightly onto the lead horse of the Duke's equipage, and set the horses off at a gallop. The footman clung for a moment, and then as they rounded a curve at great speed, fell backwards into the street. The Marquis laughed aloud for joy, and urged the horses on, springing them. As to what his bride was doing, he did not care. For all it mattered to him, she could go or stay as she liked. He would have been surprised, if he had looked inside, for she was laughing herself with amused appreciation. The protective solicitude of the men of her family, and the prospect of its continuance, had oppressed her too, fully as much as the prospective company of her reluctant husband.

The Marquis drove first directly to his Paris banker. He looked inside briefly, prepared to tell his wife grimly that he would throttle her if she screamed or tried in any way to impede him, but her face reassured him. She did not look at all like screaming. She looked much less like a mouse, and there was something in her eyes that looked surprisingly like a gleam of excitement or admiration. The Marquis found himself grinning at her, instead. He took her arm, and made his arrangements with all possible haste. When he returned her to the carriage he changed into the proper driving seat and whipped the horses off. Once outside the city, he continued at a faster pace than before. He did not stop all afternoon, except to change horses once.

By evening they were in the heart of the French countryside, among the vineyards with their vines like little crooked men, and the mountains lying far off and low against the sky. The sun's long gold rays lingeringly withdrew themselves, the air was clear and still and very peaceful. They had stopped before a small inn in a little village. Cressy, now more apprehensive, heard the door open, and the Marquis held out his hand for her to dismount. His hand closed over hers reassuringly, as he led her in, saying: "I have spoken for rooms for us, and dinner. There is no private parlour, but since there is no one here but us, we should be, I think, quite comfortable."

The Wedding

A fire burned on the hearth, and there were smells of coffee and bread and roasting meat in the air. She went up to her private room where her lighter portmanteau had been put, a small room but clean and fresh with the night air. She drew the shutters to, removed her cloak, and changed her white dress to one more suited for a country inn, and smoothed her hair. She was not frightened, for she thought that nothing any worse could come to her than had come already, only very weary, and she did not know what was in her new lord's mind.

He was standing by the window, looking out, when she came down, his face thoughtful. He turned, smiled at her with the courtesy of a stranger, and seated her. She found he meant to speak impersonally, and she followed his lead with some gratitude. They made a very good dinner, and then he went over by the fire and sat down and stretched out his legs comfortably. She did not know whether to go or stay, and so she stayed where she was. She did not know what he would say or do next, and to her surprise, she found she was not certain about her own wishes. She had hardly looked at him for himself, the past fortnight. He had moved like a puppet, as had she, but now the real man was here again, and she was aware of power and unpredictability, under his surface easy manner. He became aware of her gaze, and yawned and summoned her over to sit beside him. She looked at his face, and suddenly her heart contracted, for the lines in it looked older and sadder and more drawn, than when she first saw him in her father's study. She thought, "My father has hurt him. He may have hurt me, but he has been hurt, and more than I."

He took her hand and held it, turning the fingers over in

his; she did not try to draw it away but let it lie there, quiet, beating like a little bird's pulse. His own was cool and smooth and nerveless, without pulse. "What's to do, my dear," he said with a little smile. "Here we are." He was looking into the fire, still keeping her hand. "I know this marriage is not to your liking—neither is it to mine," he said gently. "Had things been otherwise, perhaps, who knows—but they were not and are not." He paused, and she wondered what he meant, for what his thoughts were she could not gather from his words.

"I am sorry for it, too, my lord," she said.

"Your hand is trembling," he said, and gave it back to her. "I hope you're not afraid of me?"

"I don't know who you are, my lord," she said sincerely. "That is what troubles me most."

"Would it make so much difference, if you knew?" he asked. "Wouldn't it just embarrass you more? To know the undeserved calamities you'd brought upon me, or to know a monster sits beside you?" He paused. "You'd not credit me, it would be no use to try. If I say I never saw you, if I say, I've been victimised myself, I think you'll not believe me; and believe me, I'm not going to say, 'Miss Daviot'—" he paused— "'Marchioness—I have raped you.' Come now, you know that. You'll have to learn it for yourself, what you need to think." He seemed very tired, and she forbore to trouble him further.

"Your father's made a mistake," he said. "I'm not the husband for you. I'm sorry for it, and for you; but we must make the best of it. A country squire, perhaps?" Then he asked abruptly, with one of his alarming changes of humour: "Are you pregnant? Do you know?"

She blushed. "I do not know."

"I care," he said with conscious cruelty.

"I think you're trying to hurt me," she said, rising. "I would like to go."

"Sit down," he said, and kept his stern eyes on her until she did. "You are right. I am not a kind man, they tell me."

"I think you could be, my lord," she said slowly. "The man who took me was most kind in himself, even though he was very cruel to take me as he did."

"*I'm* not going to take you," he said abruptly, standing up. "There's been enough of this. I'm demned tired. We need our sleep." He bent down and kissed her forehead gently, led her out and up the stairs, and left her at the door of her room.

He was finishing his breakfast, when she came down. He had been enjoying the simpler pleasures, which he had once taken for granted and undoubtedly would again, of walking by himself, making his own arrangements, eating peacefully what he chose in a public house. His temper was sunny, and he rose politely as she came in, and kissed her hand.

"Good morning, Marchioness. You slept well?" She thanked him; he seated her and ordered more breakfast. "I am enjoying myself without your father and his household. Demned if I was going to take all your family and family servants on my wedding trip. But you may miss them?" He surveyed her lazily, relaxed, lounging in his chair.

"I am content, my lord."

"I'd damned well think you would be," he said, suddenly vicious. "You have what you wanted, no? A name, my name? A Marquis now, someday a Duke?"

"I never wished to be your wife. I could not help myself," she answered, her face whitening under his attack.

"I think you could. I think you had it *fixed*, you and your *père*." She said nothing. "Did you not?" He repeated his questioning, more furiously yet: "Did you not?"

"I would have chosen not to wed you. There were other things I could have done, and my father would not have forced me, though I knew he wished it. But—"

"But what—?"

"He intimated he would have you killed, if I did not."

"Good lord! You believed him?"

"He felt his honour had been touched too, my lord."

"So I've been spared a duel? I'm rather good at them, I think he might have lost. He counted on Heaven's judgement?"

"Not a duel, my lord."

Suddenly he began to laugh, loudly. "By God, that's rich—I think I'm saving you, and all the time you think you're saving me?"

"Did you think it, sir?"

He paused and looked at her. "I think you have a low opinion of me, Cressy."

"Yes, my lord"—she gave him her sudden whole-hearted smile that never failed to move him—"and yet, you see, I wish you well."

"Do you, Cressy?" For a moment only he really seemed to look at her, and then the spirit vanished behind his eyes. "I half thought you would not be here this morning. I thought I'd scared you off."

"Did you try, my lord? I had nowhere I could go. When we return to England—if we do?—perhaps I can oblige you."

"I'll thank you, no. You are my own, now, and I am jealous of my property."

"We cannot keep, sir, what we do not value."

"Oh, I value *you*, Cressy, but perhaps not as you might think. I mean to keep you by me!" He looked at her, briefly amused. "So you did not wish to wed me?"

"No, my lord."

"I may beat you, if you keep on telling me that, it don't flatter me." His tone changed. "What was he like?"

"Who, my lord?"

"This man who raped you."

She choked on her coffee. "My *lord!*"

"What was he like, I say?" He stared at her with no humour in his face.

"I cannot tell, my lord. It could have been yourself. The voice, the size, was much the same. I do not know. It was a kind of—world apart. I do not think I'd know the man again. My mind has shut him out, and all that night."

"Aren't you afraid that I may do the same?"

"It is *your* right, my lord."

"You did not answer me. Aren't you afraid?"

She bowed her head and said in a low voice: "The man who taught me, taught me well: there's very little in it, without love, if there is skill. But if you take me now, when there's no love, I think you are the same as he who took me then and did not love me either."

"The same or like the same?" She shook her head. "Will you scream?"

"My lord, you *are* my lord. I do not wish you, but I must endure you."

He flushed suddenly at her remark, then he said: "Finish your breakfast, girl, and come."

"I am not hungry—" he looked at her plate quizzingly—
"this talk is hard to eat by."

"Then take yourself upstairs into *my* room." At her startled
look, he explained himself. "I mean to confuse the issue of
paternity. Or shall we do that here?" he said, taking her arm.
"The door will lock."

"I'll go, my lord." She walked up the stairs ahead of him,
her head held high. He followed, with his demon on his
shoulder.

She had not been within his room before. He came in close
behind her and locked the door. "Strip, my girl, and quickly
now." He leaned against the door, watching her negligently.

She shook her head, gasping. "I cannot, sir, when you look
at me. Are such things not better done in the dark?"

"I want to see what I have bought." He came over to her
and took hold of the neck of her dress and ripped it from her
shoulders. Suddenly, with no more warning, he thrust her
back against the wall, fastening his lips and tongue on hers,
and held her so, while he hastily pushed aside her clothing
and his own. Then pulling her down onto the floor, on top
her dress and slips, he mounted her and penetrated, roughly
and expertly and quickly. He had finished almost before he
had begun. He extricated himself, picked her up, and tossed
her on the bed, throwing the covering across her.

"Now I have made you mine, as well as he did, and you
know *my* stamp." His lip curled. "These things are easy, are
they? Was it the same?"

Her eyes were closed, and she lay, shivering and tangled in
her clothing, not moving from where he put her. Suddenly his
heart was moved with pity, and his angry calculations of mis-

leading her forgot, he took off his boots and coat and neckcloth and got in bed beside her and pulled her to his breast, and stroked her hair, and caressed her.

"Oh love," he said, "oh love, I have a fearful temper and a wicked heart, and you provoke me with your rational ways. Do not be ashamed, my love. It had to come. We know each other now. Another time you'll school me to be gentler."

"I cannot think, sir," she murmured, "how you got your reputation."

"Which?" he asked.

"As a lover? It does not seem to me deserved."

"Don't argue with me, Cressy," he said, and closed her mouth with his. "I think that I must love you after all," he said softly, almost to himself. "Whatever I may do or say, when I am not myself, as I am now, remember it. I never thought to feel this way. Do you love me?"

"How could I, sir? You ask too much."

He put an arm about her and pulled her closer. "I must teach you then—someday." Very gently then he took her disarranged clothing from her—she did not resist him—and laid her down, looking at her gravely, until she blushed, and then gently he took her again, though she protested and cried against it because he had hurt her before, softly and gently like the waves of the ocean, until they both came to rest. He stayed there for they knew not how long, resting in the peace of her, the minutes slipping by unheeded, until finally he slipped away from her.

"How do you think you will like sleeping with a man?" he asked smiling.

"I like it very much." He kissed her eyelids.

"Do you love me now?"

"No, my lord." He groaned.

"Then that will have to do." Suddenly he saw the time and the sun. "Good God! your father will have us before we are on our way. What are you doing in that bed, woman?"—she giggled and his spirits skyrocketed—"For shame, get up and dress!" He threw the cover to her and caught her hands—"I shall take you to Sienna—will you like that?—and to Florence —and to Rome. I'll buy or rent a coach and four and we will send your father's back to him. Hurry, we'll lunch, and then we'll leave this lovely Inn, which I believe is called the Beaurester." His moods changed like the lightning. "I have never been so happy, my love; remember it, for us both, I cannot promise for myself."

XI

THE RETURN

The next three months were very happy ones. They lived, and loved, and walked, and saw the sights; but all the time he never told her anything. She talked sometimes of her past life, but never he, of his. They lived entirely in the present moment, in the hot warming sun of the Italian climate and of his desire.

Sometimes they drove to little villages and climbed to half-forgotten castles and looked out from their empty windows to the far-stretching fields and plains, and imagined past armies spreading across the fertile plantings. Sometimes they rode along the Lido in the night, the horses' hooves muted in the sand, the white moonlight illuminating all the sea and land in a different day, spreading a silver path which they took and lay, clasped close, beside the glinting ripples. He had entrée to the palaces, and they walked among their treasures, and among the treasures of the churches. They strolled across the bridges that spanned the Arno, and he bought her bunches of lavender, and bracelets of silver filigree from the little shops that line the Ponte Vecchio, and watched the pink and gold sun and the green trees reflected in the arches underneath them, and the coloured fishing boats, like spiders, raising and lowering their high-flung shining nets. They ate under vine-covered trellises, the pale green grapes hanging in long clusters that nearly touched their heads, the pigeons walking up and down the ladders leaning against the walls, and talking in their own soft languages. They explored the furry ruins of Rome; the cracked tiles on the uneven floor of the old Forum, passing between the shattered capitals and lonely shafts; and the Coliseum lying abandoned like a giant's broken napkin ring. Sometimes they picnicked in the Caesars' gardens, with wine and cheese, the black umbrella pines shining like glass in the white sunshine.

He avoided his acquaintances on the Continent, but content with one another and what they saw, they did not miss for company. Neither of the two wished to remember their own world, or to have reality in the shape of past or future to intrude. They felt very little need even to talk to one another: the touch of hands, the glance of eyes, their bodies and their breaths mingled together contented them. If she knew she was more his mistress than his wife, if she knew that they were like two children playing at love, she pushed the knowledge from her. His part was the more thoughtless one: he wanted her, he took her, he found her company and the life they led enjoyable and he enjoyed both, and for the time did not regret that they had so peremptorily been brought together.

But finally, as the summer began to turn, and although only late August, a warning of fall scented the air, he turned the horses West once more, before the Channel crossing grew rougher. And so, all things unresolved, they returned to England, Cressy in her fourth month increasing. And as they neared the shores of England, some weeks later, even with the greying of the skies, the shadow that had always lain between them, grew heavier, like a cloud.

He took her first to meet his mother and his father in the country. True to his character, he did not explain or apologise for having told them nothing; and true to theirs, they did not ask. They had read of his engagement and his almost immediate foreign marriage with shock but not exactly disbelief, for they knew his unaccountable nature from long-standing acquaintance. But the marriage was unexceptionable, and his mother put away her hurt and his father his acidity, to welcome them. They knew who Cressy was, but they had never really met her. They approved her at first sight, and wondered a little how their wild son had won her. Although her father's home of Rotherby was near the seat of Adversane, the Marquis did not offer to take Cressy there, and she did not press him to. Neither did he tell his parents she was pregnant, his reasons not clearly defined even to himself, and since their visit was a short one, his parents did not guess.

Straightway then he took his wife up to his Town House in London. He sent cards to his relatives and acquaintances, they met, they briefly made the rounds. He left instructions with his servants about her relatives. He instructed Cressy otherwise to leave the servants quite alone. Her father, shortly after their return which they had not informed him of, once came to call upon her, when her husband was not there. There had been not much for them to say. He had not reproached her for not writing him, but she reproached herself, and her heart misgave her when she saw how much older his dear face had grown in those short months. His practised eye took in at once her altered condition, but he did not remark upon it. In fact, they talked of very little that might not have been as easily found in a travel guide, and more safely. Surmising his presence in the Marquis' house might involve a personal danger to himself, he did not stay long. He had no wish to see his son-in-law. But he brought himself finally to speak of what lay foremost in his thoughts.

"You are happy, Cressy?" he asked, hardly trusting his voice upon the subject. She nodded without speaking. "And no regrets?" She shook her head. The Marquis, informed by his servants, came in then, polite, reserved, meeting the Duke as almost a stranger, very much now the master in his house. The Duke did not linger, but bowed and took his leave. Neither saw reason, or had desire, for a second meeting.

And at first the Marquis behaved himself as a proper husband, but he soon grew bored. How he expected to live he had not pictured to himself, during the lovely summer; but the reality of an alien presence (for so women in essence appeared to him) continually in his own house, where he had used to be alone, displeased him. He had not wanted to be married, as he had told the Duke, and as each day passed he wished more that he was not. He hated any claim of domesticity. He had been well content with his life as he had made it for himself, and he disliked the change as much as his disapproving valet could have wished. Gradually his old life, his old friends (excepting the particular ones he had gamed with in the hell) reclaimed him. He began taking up the opium habit, fashionable in some quarters.

As Cressy grew heavier, his hours grew later. Sometimes she would meet him, plunging up for bed as she was going down the stairs, the dawn long since come. Both by her inexperience and her condition she was incapable of engaging or comprehending his mercurial and indulgent self, once his attention had passed from her. Had she been asked, and free to speak, she would have said, the Italianate memories still fresh, that he was with a mistress; for she well knew his nature, and she knew he was not using it with herself—he had not touched her since they came on English soil. But she would have been mistaken. Desire had left him, for her or anyone, woman or man. Their surroundings had brought back abruptly and painfully the days he had spent at her father's house, and all his spirit had vanished, flogged out of him by the memory now as then. The freshening miracle he had briefly felt was as if it had never been. Furthermore, he had no experience of gravid women, and he did not know how to bear himself around one. Her heaviness embarrassed and repulsed him, and he could not support the bitter thoughts her presence now put again into his mind. He knew nothing of children, and confronted with the evident fact that he was shortly to have one, he found in himself no desire for it. From day to day, their relationship deteriorated.

Some days he hardly seemed to notice she was there, and was brusque and curt when she chanced to meet him, as though she intruded into some private place. Occasionally, something she would say would rouse not the irritation or the patient endurance that hurt her and which she was powerless to penetrate, but a kind of intolerable hatred and anger flashing from his eyes, directed at her. Her instinct was to creep about the house and cower away when he was there, but any show of hurt or fear provoked him more, and so she learned to bear herself outwardly as if she were the mistress of her house, and he her husband, instead of the pretender she knew herself to be in actuality. She rarely saw him when she felt he was entirely sober, and his eyes sometimes had an abstracted, brooding gaze, or a dark turmoil within them that frightened her because she did not understand it. She looked vainly for the merry, teasing looks he had directed on her, or even his hard, appraising stares. The summer might not have been, except now she had not even the casual refuge of being in truth a stranger, with the courtesy he afforded strangers. Whole days could pass with no word between them, when his glance passed through her without seeing her. The child he never mentioned. That she carried one, and was sometimes ill, he ignored. Sometimes she thought, incredibly, he had forgotten.

Occasionally he would ask her impatiently why she did not go out, if she was bored, but she forbore to tell him that she had no friends in town, and lacked the courage and the energy in her situation to meet new faces and new experiences alone. He accepted no mutual invitations, so of course she did not either. But though she shrank from his moods and his irritable ways, never knowing when she would find him genial or withdrawn, she shrank more from the emptiness of the house, with its tall rooms and vacant ceilings, its immense doors and vast echoing halls, without him; for when he was there, at least he filled it with his presence. The sound of his voice, after a night away, suddenly speaking in the hall, the slight sound he made, clearing his throat, though in another room, oblivious of her presence, flooded her with relief, even as it pierced her with a yearning bitterer than any emotion she had ever known before, sharper even than grief. More and more, however, she found herself alone.

Before the servants, even her abigail, she kept her counsel to herself. With most of them she had little to do. The hardest person she found to deceive was Robertson, and she did not believe she had. She knew that gentlemen talked freely with their valets, that they occupied a privileged position, and were more intimate with their masters in some ways than a wife could be. She knew he disapproved strongly of their sudden marriage out of England, and particularly resented that he had been left behind, both from the Marquis' visit to Rotherby and subsequent travels on the Continent. His voice conveyed towards her a kind of well-bred sneer to which she could not take exception, for he had been in the house long before her, and he implied, she thought, would be there after.

When the child began moving within her, she was frightened, but the Marquis was unconcerned. "Something wrong inside you? I'd see a doctor, then, my dear. Try Hartley, he should do." He did not ask her about the outcome of her visit, but after that her only joy, as well as her apprehension, came from the little creature within her that she could feel. Her father came a second time to see her, but she took no pleasure in his visit, for she could see the displeasure and concern on his face. She did not want his pity, or his concern, and she defended her absent husband to him. But she thought he was not fooled. "She would go out in society after the baby was born," she told him, "when she felt easier." She could see her being alone alarmed him for her safety.

"Gore should be home, or hire an experienced woman to stay with you," he said. "Or use your own moneys, my dear," he advised. "You are well along, and something could occur when you're alone, and you'd be helpless." But he was helpless to manage the affairs of her or her husband in her husband's home.

As the year drew on to November and Advent, towards the joyous season, there was no mirth in their house. No change occurred, except the Marquis stayed away from home for longer intervals more frequently, and she grew very large. She was in her seventh month now. Cressida's father arrived one morning when his lordship, absent several days, was still not returned, to find his daughter in tears, her defenses quite down. Definite stories of her solitude and her husband's manner of life had reached him, and he had come expressly to find out what truth was in them. But he did not need to ask. She let him take her in his arms, and sobbed out her anxiety. He comforted her as best he could, hiding the shock he felt at the change in her, at her listlessness and the despair in her wan face. He knew she was within some few weeks of her time, and he was both angered and frightened. He attempted to persuade her to leave the house and come to his, but she would not. He then began to put in motion certain enquiries.

XII

THE DUEL

One evening in November the Marquis went for the first time to the new hell where his former four friends were now playing cards. They looked at him self-consciously, but his face showed no embarrassment. He went straight to the point.

"Viscount, where is your black box, do you keep it by you? Yes, I see it. You owe me money, several thousand lou, I do believe: a hasty marriage, and a babe. You do remember?" he asked sweetly. At their astonished faces, he added, "It was not said to whom. I cannot see that the marriage being made to me should cancel out the stake."

"Lord, Gore, I always said you'd do anything to win a bet," said the Honourable Frederic approvingly.

The Viscount Lisle paid the large stack out, without comment. Then he said: "We've missed you, Gore. Does being a married man make you so sober you neglect old friends?"

The Marquis gave a hard laugh. "God, I'm not sober, ask around, but I prefer to drink and play with friends." He looked at each one of the four searchingly, ponderingly.

The Honourable Frederic said, "I say, I protest that remark!"

"And I say," the Marquis replied, "that one here is not my friend. And I believe," he said slowly, "that it is Teviot here, who told my *beau-père* my *petite histoire.*"

His guess proved a good one, for Teviot stood up, his cheeks blanched, his hands shaking slightly. Barely twenty, he was much under the Viscount Lisle's influence, but his years at times betrayed him. "You lie, Gore, I did not," he said with trembling lips.

"Did not what? What did you not? Say I 'lie'? I don't as a rule let men or boys say I lie—not with my hands free," he added, for his own benefit, remembering. "You will prove that point with me, or tell me, and us all, how precisely you informed his Grace of Salisbury?"

"I shall prove it then," Teviot said, with some show of bravery, for publicly confess he could not. The Marquis counted on that. He did not wish a confession, he wanted an excuse to kill him.

"With swords, then, or with pistols? Either will do me."

"The pistols will do," Teviot said whitely.

"Pistols then. Frederic, will you second me?"

After some arrangements, and the sending for Teviot's pistols (his lordship had brought his own with foresight), they withdrew to a secluded green, not taking time to find and wake a surgeon, and measured off, and fired. The Marquis lost a lock of hair, which was shot off, but the young man Teviot fell with a severe wound in his chest.

The Marquis walked over, and looked down at him without emotion. "Is he dead?"

The Viscount Lisle, Teviot's second, in near tears, replied angrily: "Nearly! Frederic, fetch a surgeon! We came in too much stupid haste, without one. It is irregular, Gore, as you well know. That won't go well, if Teviot dies."

"If? I thought it a sure thing. Next time I will make it one, I hope."

"He's just a boy, Bysshe!" the Honourable Frederic expostulated.

"If he's a boy, let him stay home with his mother. If he's a man, let him act a man then," said the Marquis angrily, walking off.

Teviot raised himself, from his faint, and tried to speak. Lord Herriot, catching the almost indistinguishable words, called to the Marquis to come back: "Gore, Teviot wants to speak to you."

"He's spoken to me, as I remember. I've nothing more to say." Nevertheless, the Marquis halted.

"Bysshe!" The young man faltered out his name with an urgent appeal. The Marquis turned slowly—he could hardly hear the boy. "Bysshe," he said very weakly, "I did not want to, but—she was my cousin."

The Marquis looked as horrified as he was. He reversed his plans rapidly. "We'll take him to a surgeon, in my coach, it will be quicker so, though harder on him," he said briefly. He took off his coat, then his shirt, and put his coat back on and wadded up his shirt to make a pad, which he pressed against the wound, hopelessly attempting to stop the flow of blood. Between them they carried him to the coach. Teviot had fainted again before they reached a surgeon.

They wakened the sleeping doctor as discreetly as they might. The Marquis saw the young man taken into the surgeon's room with his two friends, and left, but he did not go home. Instead he walked, through the grey November London streets, aimlessly, his thoughts not clear to himself. Several times he went back to hear the surgeon's report, but the only report was that there was nothing to report, no change. The young man might live or he might die.

The Marquis, impatient, called on his family's physician, and on his recommendation, on another surgeon, one he knew by reputation, not by use. Together they succeeded in removing the young man to his father's house and put him comfortably to bed, with his mother and his sister, holding back their anger and their grief, to watch him. On the way there, the Marquis sat beside Teviot in the coach. The boy lay motionless, looking as pale as if he were already dead.

Once, over a rough jolt, his eyes flew open, and widened in terror at the sight of the Marquis' grim face. His lips soundlessly parted, and then he gasped: "Come to finish—, Bysshe? Not—hard—"

The Marquis took his hand and held it in his. Tears, unexpectedly, rose behind his eyes, and he said unsteadily: "I had as soon kill myself—You were a fool not to tell me what your reason was, before we fought."

"Ashamed," the boy said faintly.

"I didn't know it, Charles. I don't shoot family—not a usual thing for me."

"I—loved her, Bysshe. Do you?"

The Marquis did not answer. He held the boy's hand firmly in his grip. "When you get well of this, Charles, we'll have a dinner, you, my wife, all of us."

Teviot did not answer. Alarmed, the Marquis felt his pulse, but thought he found life in him. The second surgeon was waiting at Teviot's father's house, his things in readiness. He looked severely at the Marquis.

"Where shall I find you, if you're wanted?" he asked, with meaing in his voice.

"I shall be here, or at my home."

"They do not want you here."

"Then at my home, or I shall seek you out."

He did not want to go home—and he did not want company. He went to one of the hotels, and took a room there, and fell asleep. He did not wake until afternoon. He sent round to Teviot's house again, and ordered lunch while he waited. The servant returned, saying that he could get no report; and the Marquis sent him out again to his valet, asking him to bring a change of clothes. Then he went round himself by the surgeon's house, again, and got no definite report. He had killed men in duels before, without a qualm, and this dead anxiety weighing him down was new to him. He could not explain it to himself. His thoughts were not moving quickly, and although Cressy was at the root of the affair, oddly he gave no thought to her anxiety, or to her at all.

XIII

THE NINTH EPISODE

THE LEAVE-TAKING

Cressida was sitting in the small salon, in the low spirits that now generally beset her, when her older brother, Kit, was announced. She had not seen him since her wedding.

"Where's Gore?" he asked at once, without ceremony. "Has he been in last night?"

"I-I have not seen him," she answered evasively. "Wh-why do you ask?"

He did not notice her own distress in the rigour of his feelings. "My—our—cousin Charles was killed—shot—last night—this morning—and someone said he had a duel with Gore—but it's devilish hard somehow to find out anything. I want to know where Gore is, I want to talk to him."

"Oh, no!" she cried, horrified, "Charles is not killed?"

"I don't know for sure," he said more accurately, "it's very serious. They're telling different things."

"Can't you go to Charles' house?"

"He isn't there, he's at his father's, and they're not answering the door. The place is in a roar about it. Where's Gore—is he here?"

"I-I don't think so. I haven't looked—"

"Well, *look* then; isn't it your house?" He eyed her curiously. As she paused, he said, anxiously: "Cressy, don't you *know?*" She bit her lip a little. He pressed her relentlessly. "When did you see him last? When was he last home?"

"I'm not sure," she faltered. "Yesterday, I think."

"You *think?*"

"Kit, please go now; when I see my lord, I will tell him you want to see him. You make me feel unwell and duller than my usual." She spoke with a piteous dignity that undid him. He kissed her hand, and bowed, and left.

He went straight to his father and said the situation was impossible—and several other things besides.

"It is what I think myself," his father interposed quietly.

Kit continued expostulating for several moments before he realised what had been said. "You agree?" he said, incredulous.

"I agree. Come near and let me tell you what I think ought to be done. This last shooting of young Teviot is not only an intolerable affront, it gives me the excuse to do at once what I've been thinking necessary." He added, with sincere interest: "Why, by the way, do you think they duelled? Did Gore shoot him because he is my nephew, or did they have real matter for a quarrel?"

"I do not know for sure Gore shot him."

"I do. His father told me. The Viscount Rockfort told him

part of it, for he was there, with Lisle, as Teviot's second, but he did not divulge the reason, if he knew it."

"How is Teviot?"

"Very low. They expect he will not live the night."

"Good Lord!" Kit said fervently. "Gore is half a dozen years the older, and twice the experienced. He must have shot to kill."

"The Viscount thinks he did. I'm wondering why." The Duke spoke with a deceptive mildness.

But he took no more time for wondering, but took himself to the Marquis' house, to sit with his daughter. She had collected herself, and she presented a braver front to him, despite her distress at her cousin's predicament. He was there when the note came for the Marquis' valet. He intercepted it from the footman, but he did not deliver it. Despite Cressy's attempts to retain it, he kept her away, and took his glass, and perused it carefully.

"I shall go speak to Gore, myself," he said, "and then I will myself report back to you." The tone of his voice invited no argument.

"But his valet?"

"He shall have the message on my return, if Gore still wishes it." He left, leaving her still in ignorance of her husband's whereabouts.

Although it was only shortly after four, the late November dusk was falling. With his two sons and his servant, his Grace quietly let himself into the Marquis' apartments. The Marquis was sitting stretched out in front of the fire, half hidden in a large armchair. He had fallen off into a light sleep. He heard vaguely the door that he had left on latch for his valet, and spoke a drowsy word of greeting. Then, without other warning, a dark smotheringly soft piece of material was thrown over his head, and hands pulled and held him back against the chair, while a length of rope was wound round and round his shoulders and arms and legs. When he struggled, the brown blanket-like folds were pulled close. He could hardly breathe, and the sensation was so unpleasant, he made no further resistance, only trying to find air left in the folds. He was lifted up, like a child, his face pushed against some-one, and something else fell on his shoulders, his travelling cloak he later realised. Arms of enormous strength, like a bear's, held him clutched so close he could not have moved, had he tried. A door opened, closed, he heard voices, faintly. Then he was put inside some kind of chaise, and the vehicle moved off. A moment later, the smothering cloth was pulled down from his face, and he gasped in the night air, not bothering immediately to look at his assailants. He had thought it must be an act of friends of Teviot, and he was surprised to see his Grace of Salisbury sitting across from him, and on either side of him one of Cressy's brothers. He recognised then the grip of his Grace's prize-fighting servant, Bernard.

"I'd think that you'd get tired of this," the Marquis said wearily.

"I do. It is for the last time," his Grace said evenly. He spoke without expression, but the words chilled the Marquis so, he did not answer, or attempt to make rejoinder.

After a time, though, he ventured to ask: "Where are we going? Is it far?"

"Quite far."

"I see," the Marquis said; he thought he did see, and he did not ask any more. After a moment, he said quietly: "I would like then—if I may—to say good-by to my wife."

"I'm afraid that is not possible."

"I beg you to make it possible," the Marquis said sincerely, in a low voice. The coach was dark, but his Grace, in surprise, saw what looked to be tears glistening in the Marquis' eyes and on his cheeks.

"What will you say to her?" he asked curiously.

"I will say 'good-by,'" said the Marquis simply. "I have not seen her now since—oh," he said in an exhausted voice, "I cannot remember now. Not today, I know. She's having a child," he added unnecessarily, "I wouldn't want her to really worry, that might injure her—or the child—or both of them, you see."

The horses rode on in the dark of early evening, towards the outskirts of London. The Marquis made no further appeal. His Grace pondered what the Marquis had said, and the manner of its delivery.

"I find your lack of speech more eloquent than your words," he said finally. Then he asked, a little incredulously: "You think she'd care?"

"With women who's to know?" The Marquis shrugged. "Perhaps, perhaps not. I do not know." He hardly seemed interested any longer.

"You are then reconciled?" the Duke asked.

"It seems I must be." He smiled faintly. "I cannot help myself."

"What will you say?" the Duke asked once again, this time practically.

"I thought I'd say I had to go somewhere—on business. Reassure her now. Then you can do the rest, some later time, more gently, when you think it's time." He spoke very slowly, stopping between phrases.

"Your looks would hardly reassure her. When did you last shave?"

"I sent for my valet, some time ago. He did not come. You can take me by your house—or by my own. It will be the same."

His Grace nodded. "As you wish, then, Gore, in this." He called out to the coachman to turn back.

"Does Teviot live?" the Marquis asked.

"I do not know. I think not."

"Tell Cressy, for the moment he improves, I think." They drove on without speaking. It was eight when they arrived at the Marquis' door.

"Come in with me," the Marquis invited unnecessarily. Then in a quick low voice he said: "Let me lead. I will not trick you. You will find I give you no cause for regret. But leave those brothers out here. Tell them to walk ahead, we'll pick them up. They can dine at White's. Will she know your coach?"

"I have rented this equipage," the Duke replied. Only the Marquis' eyes registered that he understood the import of this information.

The next hour incited the Duke to admiration for the Marquis, although he could not like him. He called to his wife that he was home, but not yet shaved, and that her father waited for her below. Then he closeted himself with his valet, and half an hour later, emerged more like himself, though in dark travelling clothes.

"Cressy, may we dine?" he said, not really asking. "Are we too late?" He could see traces of tears on her cheeks and guessed her anxiety during the afternoon, but he thought to ignore them. After some hurried kitchen stir, they dined well, even pleasantly, so that a brighter look and some colour came back into Cressy's bereft face; talking formally until they reached the Marquis' unfrequented library, and the servants went out and closed the door.

The Duke engaged himself at looking through the books on the Marquis' shelves with carefully fixed attention. The Marquis crossed to his wife, where she was sitting, and took her hands, and said: "I ask your pardon, madame, in this matter of your cousin. We quarrelled. I did not learn he was your cousin —until I had wounded him. But I have hopes he will recover, and I have already asked him to dine with us when he is fit again." He smiled at her encouragingly for a moment, before his eyes grew serious again. "He is young, but he stands well, and I much regret my part. I did the most I could for him, after I discovered his relationship to you, with surgeons —I think he is in the best of hands."

She was surprised by his care for her opinion. "But if he dies—" she faltered, "what for you?"

"We will think of that when it occurs. It depends on several things." He smiled reassuringly at her. "At the worst, I might need to leave London for a while. And that's what I have to do in any case."

The colour left her face. "Leave London now?"

"Only for a short while, my dear. I have an uncle who died last week up in the North. I have just received word of it, and that his affairs are entangled. It is a coil, but I shall have to journey up and see what I can make of them."

"Cannot your father go?"

He shook his head. "I am the heir, alas."

"I wish I might come, too."

"It would not suit you nor the child.—You are so very dull here?" She nodded. "While I am gone, take your abigail and go to see your father."

She was surprised at his suggesting it, but she only said: "I would rather go to visit your mother, my lord. She has asked me, and a woman's company would cheer me very much."

He was touched. "Why, go there then, by all means. In fact, visit whom you like, if it is near. I'll find you, on my return, here or in the country."

"When do you go?" she asked fearfully.

"It must be tonight, I'm afraid."

"Tonight!" She gave a little cry. "Oh, surely you need not go tonight. You have just come back!" She caught at his hands which he had attempted to draw away. Her voice shook, but she attempted to control it, and not to provoke him with signs of her distress. "Stay only a few days."

He shook his head. "I may not stay. These affairs press me."

"And your affairs here? They are sadly out of order."

"They must wait." He saw how large the child within her had grown, and he was shocked. He had hardly looked at her the past month, even when he had been home. "They will perhaps do just as well without me." He kissed her lips lightly, and tried to make his leavetaking, but she clung to him, his hands.

"I am so afraid when you are gone," she said pleadingly.

His face showed surprise, but he was helpless to comfort her, and he did not respond, except to say, reminding her: "Your father's here and watching you. Be brave, my dear, and smile for him and me."

She smiled a little, but her tears were close. He seemed to her suddenly already somehow very remote. "Then be cross with me, and scold me, Bysshe. When you are gentle like this, you quite undo me. You must frown."

He shook his head slightly. "Frown at you? I cannot. It is you who are to frown at me," he said, with an attempt at a smile. "I have been gone too long—I know it—and now I must go again." He disengaged her hands and kissed them, and his hands and voice for a moment lost their own steadiness: "Your pardon, madame," he said softly, "for all my sins." Then, in a commonplace voice, so that she wondered if she had really heard the words just past, he gave some instructions to her about the household, sent for his valet, who was outraged to learn he must stay behind, sent him to pack for a brief journey, spoke to his groomsman about his horses, and then once more, with her father, took his leave, more formally.

What it cost him to walk from his wife and his unborn child, his valet, his servants and his household about him at his call, and to leave alone with her father, casually, his Grace only guessed at. If it cost him, he showed none of it. He paused to send a wave, and bent, and entered the coach.

"My compliments," said his Grace, not mentioning that he had had his pistol cocked the whole time in his pocket. Had the Marquis broken his word, he had intended to shoot him, but he did not tell him that. He had seated himself, and had directed Bernard, his temporary coachman, to strap the Marquis' knees together. They turned a corner, out of view of the house. The Marquis said nothing. He kept his gaze fixed ahead. His face was like glass, that might shatter at a sound.

"That was an affecting scene," the Duke said politely. "Did you expect to move me?"

The Marquis shook his head slowly and held out his hands to let the Duke bind them as before. "My word no longer holds," he said. "I will leave you if I can."

The Duke smiled at the notion. "Thank you," he said ironically, "I shall take care to see you do not."

At White's, they stopped to take up the two brothers. Kit and Timothy had heard rumour there that Teviot had died the hour before. The Marquis made no attempt to enter their conversation. It was his belief that they intended to take him some way out of town and shoot him and leave him by the road. With the highwaymen abounding, such an accident would be unquestioned. He did not expect them to fight him, for they would know he would likely win. But time passed and nothing was done.

"How long must I wait?" he asked, finally. "I would have it over with, since there is no help."

His Grace looked at him, faintly perplexed. "We have first to reach the coast. It will all take some time."

"Can you not do it here as well?"

His Grace laughed, but without mirth. "I read your mind, now, but that is not my way." With that the Marquis had to be content.

They drove steadily all through the night, stopping only to exchange their horses. The Marquis was not allowed to leave the coach, or walk about—one of the brothers Kit or Timothy, sometimes both, always remained with him. He waited patiently, looking for any laxness, but he found none. His spirits were already low, and he gave in finally to their depression.

XIV

THE DEPARTING

Nevertheless, the smell and sound of the sea came as a shock to the Marquis. It had not occurred to him that it really might be his Grace's intention to take him out of the country, even though he had himself suggested it as perhaps a necessity to his wife, and he could not conceive his purpose in so doing.

A yacht was waiting for them which the Marquis did not recognise; the tide was up and going out. With no waiting, they proceeded at once to board. The Duke had changed the binding of his lordship's hands, inside the coach, to secure them, less noticeably, behind him, and had draped his cloak about him and fastened it.

As he released the Marquis' knees, the Duke remarked: "It will make no difference really what you happen to say or do here. This is Kit's yacht that we sent ahead to have brought round and readied."

This information surprised the Marquis, for he had thought that all the Duke's anger had to do with the killing of his nephew, which was cause enough though not uncommon. He had not imagined plans of any such complication as he now saw, exceeding in time back beyond the duel. But the implications of his abduction and his Grace's manner could not be made more sinister than they already were, although the manner of the final disposition puzzled him. What it might be he could not imagine. He wondered if he was to be dropped, helpless and bound, into the cold sea in the middle of the crossing; or first some way killed and then dropped, to simulate an accident, should his body wash up on shore. It all seemed overly involved. But his depression was so acute, and the fatigue of the last days so numbing, he found himself not really caring. He only hoped he should continue not to care.

The morning sky was grey but the sea was calm, despite the season; the journey promised to be a pleasant one for anyone spending it on deck. The Marquis spent the six hours below in a small cabin, with one of the three men, or their servant, taking turns to stay with him. He sat down on the cabin's cot and leaned back against the wall. His humour did not conduce to idle wit or exchanges, and his pride forbade him to ask any questions. His Grace had no words at all, and Kit, the older twin, even less—but Timothy was as usual without embarrassment.

"Ain't you the least sorry about Teviot?" he asked.

"Is he indeed dead?" asked the Marquis heavily. "Is there no possibility of a mistake?"

"Well, you don't as a rule leave much of one, when you shoot a man, Gore. I was surprised he was not dead right off. Do you care?"

"We were friends, of a sort," the Marquis said.

"Well, Lord, then, why did you shoot him at all? Couldn't you just overlook him, as a raw pup?"

"It seemed the thing to do, at the time," said the Marquis, "but times change. I do wish now I hadn't. I would give half my year's rents to have him still alive."

"I dessay you do. But honestly, I don't think it would change my father's mood. He's in a taking. It's just a kind of excuse, you know, the last insult, or something. He's had this fixed for some weeks now." He flushed. "Lord, I talk too much."

"I think you do. What has your father fixed?"

"I mustn't tell you. Well, I'm not even absolutely sure. I'm sorry for you, though, Gore. I am. I think my father's rather rough. I mean, I know it was dishonourable, and you're so arrogant one likes to take you down—but Hell, my sister always liked you, so what's the difference in the end?"

"Did she?" The Marquis looked startled. "How do you know that?"

"Oh, I could tell. Kit doesn't notice things like that, he was always thinking about his own plans and what he wanted. I mean, Hell, it was years ago—and we didn't see you much after we left school, but after you visited us one Christmas, her ears would prick up for our stories about school when you figured in them. I shouldn't tell you this."

"No, it makes no difference, does it?" the Marquis agreed with a twisted smile. "It's odd, you know, I never noticed her. Not to speak of, that is. I have a memory for trifles, but I never thought a little girl like that saw who her brothers went about with."

"Lord, don't they just! You're supposed to know a deal about the women, Gore, but I see you hadn't any sisters."

"No, nor brothers either—until now."

"Well, I don't think you'd better count on us as brothers, Gore, for this is not the way I'd do to Kit, no matter what he'd done or what m'father said."

"But you are twins," the Marquis commented. Timothy's easy confidences led him to ask the question in his mind. "What's it about, Tim, do you know? If it's not young Teviot, as I made sure it was, and that's good cause, I think, what is it I'm supposed now to have done?"

Timothy looked embarrassed. "I think my father thinks you haven't treated Cressy very well. I think he just thinks she'd be better off without you."

"Has Cressy told him so?"

He looked even more embarrassed. "I wouldn't know."

"Well, has she?" asked the Marquis again, more sharply. Even situated as the Marquis was, Timothy found him a difficult man to refuse.

"Hell, Bysshe," said Timothy, goaded, "I ain't going to read you a lecture here. Do *you* think you've treated her well? You'd know better than I would if she had any cause to."

The Marquis absorbed this answer silently. Then he looked up, and asked practically: "Well, why don't she divorce me then? Or separate?"

"My father's thought of that, but that's a shame for her, and he won't have it, Bysshe. You ought to know that. He's as arbitrary as yourself, though he don't look it."

"Yes, I have cause to know."

"Teviot was sweet on Cressy, too, once—did you know?"

"He mentioned it—the other day."

"You didn't shoot him, just for that, did you, Bysshe? I mean, he was fifteen or sixteen, and hardly shaving."

"Did Cressy love him, too?"

"No, she just teased him, like another brother. It was you she had the tendre for, I told you so, at least I always thought it. You were on the Continent the year when she came out, weren't you?"

"I don't remember."

"Well, I do. Things have been in such a mess. I wish my mother hadn't died. She could keep my father's temper down. Lord, the beltings he has given us!"

"But you love him?"

"We all do. You would yourself, if you saw his other side."

"I cannot imagine it, but I will take your word for it." He looked at his voluble guard. "Timothy, will you untie my hands, and let me try my luck in the sea? I think it might be preferable to your father's kindness."

"Lord, no! It would be worth my skin, and I don't love you, Gore."

"It was just a thought," the Marquis said absently.

Timothy looked at him with a certain compassion, and said: "If I were you, Gore, I'd tell my father I was sorry about it all—"

The Marquis looked back at him quizzically.

"You know what I mean. I'd ask his pardon."

"His?" the Marquis intervened softly, but Timothy ignored him.

"He is not a hard man, when he is not crossed." He considered the matter. "Though it may be too late now, anyway. But you could try."

"I would rather die than do that," the Marquis said simply.

"Well, I wouldn't," said Timothy, eying him queerly.

"It is not your pride involved," the Marquis explained quietly. "I have been much abused by your father; it is for him, I think, to ask mine, and not me, his."

"Well, if you think so, but I would, you know," said Timothy. "Don't say I didn't try," he added comfortably, and somewhat cryptically.

His brother Kit came down the narrow stairwell then, and Timothy went back on deck. The Marquis laid himself down with care, turning his back on his new guard, and tried to compose himself to sleep. The wind freshened, as the afternoon came on, and the cabin rocked unpleasantly. They shared the common wish to be on deck. Things continued tediously so until after a long time his Grace the Duke came down to replace his elder son.

The Marquis seemed to have fallen asleep. The Duke walked over to the shipbunk and looked down thoughtfully at his unhappy sleeping guest. But what his thoughts were he did not visibly disclose. He sat down in the cabin's chair and took out a book from his greatcoat pocket and began to read. If he noticed when his guest woke, he showed no sign, but continued his reading without interruption. The Marquis sat up with difficulty and looked at his host, in his turn, consideringly.

Without raising his eyes, his Grace said, "I'm more than twice your age, Gore; you'll find it hard to put me out of countenance."

"It must be, sir, I should not try," the Marquis agreed politely, not removing his gaze. The Duke's eyes briefly flickered on his, then his Grace returned to his book and did not look up again.

"What is the book you read, sir?" the Marquis asked, after a time.

"It is a report on the state of France, written by an English visitor to the Court, this winter past," said the Duke dispassionately.

"You have friends there, perhaps?"

"I have, perhaps," the Duke said, discouraging conversation.

"Would you read to me from it?" asked the Marquis. The Duke looked surprised. "The time does not go fast here," the Marquis explained.

"If you like," his Grace said; and for the remainder of the voyage, without comment, read steadily aloud in his calm dry voice, until the sea worsened in a way that indicated they were approaching the mouth of the harbour. The Duke stayed below until the yacht was moored, then he adjusted the sea cloak over the Marquis' shoulders, and escorted him up the narrow stairs.

The wind was fresh, and the waves snapping, but the golden light of early evening lay on the wide browning fields of France. The Marquis found it inexpressibly beautiful, bursting so on his eyes, and he wondered how long he should yet see it. They took dinner in a small Inn on the Quai, in a private room, while the Duke with some difficulty learned of a coach and four he might rent for the remainder of his trip. It was dark before they began. They slept fitfully and uneasily in the coach, but the Duke did not pause except at the post houses, to change his horses.

When the light began to break, the Duke leaned forward

and bound a dark scarf over the Marquis' eyes without explanation. The Marquis, for one smothering moment of panic,
partly induced by Timothy, considered throwing himself at
his Host's feet, but he was stopped from it largely by the quick
reflection that his Grace would undoubtedly only laugh at
him, just as he had been amused by any earlier signs of distress, and imperturbably proceed as he had always intended.
To be shamed, as well, he thought, would be unendurable.
So he said nothing, and if his companions noticed the desperation in the line of his mouth, they said nothing either. The
uncomfortable journey, in close confinement, his aching arms,
the uncertainty and the waiting for what he did not know, the
darkness of the night, and now this suddenly, irrationally
induced darkness muffling out the lovely light of morning,
with its mists and hazes rising, had finally broken his nerve.
He knew it, and all that remained to him was a resolution to
not let it be known by anyone else.

So he did not see the golden city of Paris spread out before
them, nor the slow journey through the empty streets, though
he heard the cobblestones underfoot, and smelled the city
noises. He did not see the towering dark mass of building
before which they stopped, but he heard the crash of iron
doors as they entered, he heard the Duke tell his sons curtly to
wait outside, and such smells as he had never met assaulted his
nose, his mouth, his very breath. He believed then that he
would have turned and left his pride and promised the Duke
anything at all to have been taken out and away, from whatever fate waited him in this cold foreign place. But the Duke
without a word had gone, and an alien heavy hand was on his
arm, compelling him to move forward. The Duke, unknown

to him, was not far away, arranging matters of finance and detail, but the new hands led the Marquis on and out, through other crashing doors, down other cold, foetid passages, and finally forced him to bow his head under a door and enter a smaller room. The cord on his wrists was cut, the scarf about his eyes unmuffled, from behind, and without word, his still unseen conductor had gone, slamming the heavy door to and turning the clashing lock.

The light was dim in the room, or small apartment. Although there was an inner window, at first the Marquis' eyes registered nothing; then he saw a wooden table with a chair pulled up to it, and he sat down. Never, in his worst imaginings, had he considered such a fate, such an action being done to him. He could not at first assimilate it. It seemed to him out of proportion in its hideousness to anything he might have done, on friendly homely soil. His courage had completely left him, and he put down his head on the rough boards of the table and sobbed. Had the Duke made use of the peephole in the door, and seen the effects so soon of his handiwork, it is likely he would have called a halt to them. But he had been given no reason to imagine them; and having settled the arrangements, he had already left, and started with his shocked sons on his journey home.

Time passed, and the Marquis did not move. He lay like one already dead, and in this silent, lonely, tomb-like place, all unprepared, unconfessed, he felt death and that death had him. In fact, it seemed preferable to the reality of what his life had become. The shadows changed and lengthened, the dimness became more dim, and turned to blackness. It was the blackness that roused him and made him start, and look

around, to see nothing. Not even sky, for the window gave on
a court and after a space opened on another wall. He thought
for a moment that he would go mad, but even as he thought
it, he pushed it away from him. To be mad in such a place
would be unendurable. He sat up, and held his aching head,
and tried to hold his reason in him. He could do nothing in
the dark, nothing until something or someone indicated some
meaning to him in this meaningless abyss into which he had
been cast without warning. Hatred suddenly came to his aid,
hatred for his wife, his unborn child, his father-in-law, his
brothers-in-law—these people who had willed him here, heed-
lessly, while they would go on with their own lives where they
had always been. He clutched at the hatred, and nourished
himself by it.

A crashing of the lock at the low door brought him back to
the present moment. The door opened, with the glimmering
of a candle, a blessed light, and a dwarfish man came in. Behind him, he could see the feet and legs of some other man or
keeper, sworded, waiting.

"I am late with your light, I apologise, monsieur," the creature said, with a grin that struck him in the candlelight as
horrible, like a devil properly belonging in this Hell. The
dwarf ambled to the table, and set the candle down. "It was
due in here an hour ago, but we were busy with your arrival.
We expected you, but not so soon."

"You expected me?" the Marquis said with faint lips. His
past life seemed to have fallen away from him, and nothing
left to him except this incredible present. He nerved himself
to ask: "What am I here for?"

"*Pardon, monsieur?*"

"On what charge?"

"Dieu sait," the creature said, "we don't; we never ask."

"Shall I be here long? Do you know that?"

"Dieu sait," the creature only said again, smiling with its twisted lips.

"Have I been brought here to be killed?" He managed to form the words. Death on the highroad or on the duelling field or even in the sea he could contemplate if not with equanimity, with sangfroid—but the prospect of it in this death-like place—of being strangled in his sleep and left, or taken out into one of these stone corridors and butchered, overwhelmed his spirit.

"Du tout, monsieur, du tout," the little dwarf said reassuringly, "oh, no such thing! You're here to be our guest, and you'll be treated well, for there's money that's been left here for you. That's how you have the candle, and one will be bringing in your dinner any moment now. We haven't many such as you that are here right now, and we've time enough to tend to you. One is leaving, by a way you're not here for, a nicer room, with a proper window in it, and a larger space, and then we'll move you there. You'll find it much more to your liking."

His dinner now was handed in, not palate-pleasing but adequate, with a green wine to drink. He ate and drank, without relish and with no return of his spirits. He looked at the arrangements of the room, and at the bed in the corner, and hoped without much hopefulness that it was clean of creatures. He was too unhappy to wonder who had been in it last or what had happened to him, or to her, or to follow the journey of his relatives home, or to picture his house and what his wife and his servants might be thinking or doing. He was exhausted of all material and spiritual resources, and he laid himself down on the hard low bed, with its frowsy blankets, like a bereft child, tearless, his eyes open, and let sleep take him. It would not be until some days later that his baffled brain would realise that the Duke had somehow availed himself, through his connections, of a *lettre de cachet*, and thereby put his annoying son-in-law out of his life.

XV

THE WAITING

The next week, the Marquis was invited to come out, by the dwarf. During that time, he had seen no one, except the dwarf twice a day with breakfast and dinner, and his candle, escorted by the waiting, sworded legs. The monotony of the time was such as to defy description of it. Now, led with his eyes free down the high cold grey corridors to his new apartment, he still saw no one and heard no one, only the vast soundless emptiness of the pile. But he realised finally, and it quenched all hope from him, that he himself would not ever possibly be able to release himself from this fortress place. He found a fire burning in his new apartment, which was a welcome addition his other room had lacked, and he had felt its lack in the cold grey damp late November days and nights.

"Fires be only for the gentry, that knows how to treat

them," the dwarf confided in him," and won't go setting themselves and their rooms afire, for they knows that nothing comes of it, except we comes, and puts 'em back in rooms that be without fires. They be for them that's here to stay and live, not here for questions."

"I shall be most careful," the Marquis promised. "I am most grateful for it." He walked over to it and stood near it, appreciating a warmth he had lacked for a week. He held out his fingers and rubbed them, and almost smiled.

"It always takes them this way," the dwarf commented, approvingly, with his terrible grimace of a smile.

Though one room, the apartment was large enough to encourage walking, even leaping, and the window, although small and high and heavily barred, was an outside window that gave onto the sky. After the dwarf had gone, the Marquis pulled first the table and then the chair below it and by standing on both was able to look near the edge, but to his initial disappointment, he could see nothing but the sky. But he was content, since he had to be, to have sky, since before he had had only grey wall. It was grey sky now, with a white powdery snow blowing past. He discovered a small shelf of books that had been left by some other occupant of the room. He did not like to think about these other occupants, how they lived or where they were, but in time he thought he might find himself grateful to imagine anything at all to think about.

And so began the unchanging monotony of his new life, its days and nights sealed off from any but the most distant, unrecognisable sounds, or the immediate grinding and clashings of his door. About these months, what was there to say˙

He cursed and wept and somehow lived, or rather life lived
on—and after a time the money left ran out. Either the Duke
forgot to send more, or it miscarried, or he never intended it.
Whatever the reason, when that occurred, what amenities he
had been given vanished with the money—the fire, the candle,
the larger room, the window and its changing scrap of sky, the
visits from the dwarf. He was taken down to a lower, smaller
room, with another dim inner window; lower, he knew, because he could hear trampings and heavy sounds from time to
time above him. His dinners became mere scraps in dirty
bowls, his wine water; it was handed through the slotted grate
in the door that opened, and he handed his leavings back
through it. The door itself was not opened again.

He missed the fire, but not intolerably, for when this change
happened, it was late spring. One might have said that now
the bitterness, the iron of his imprisonment was come home
to him, except that had happened long months before, on the
first night of it. He had since seen no reason to think differ-
ently. A fire, a candle, a dinner had helped his body to survive
the cold winter in the cold stones. But his spirit had withdrawn that first night. This imprisonment brought him no
nobility of soul, no greatness of heart, no reaching of the
spirit, no attainment of philosophy. Neither Christmas nor
Easter penetrated the place where he was.

"Time is, time was, time will be," he remembered from the
sundial at his father's house, but that was in another world.
Here, he lived without time, outside it, forgotten by it, even
his hunger and its satisfaction irregular, without rhythm,
without time. The world was twilight for him, or dark; there
was no day. The emotions of love and hate, desire, anxiety, he

had forgotten; they had no meaning where he was. He did not think of his wife, or his parents, or wonder about his child. Their spirits did not visit him.

Such absolute withdrawal had been gradual, over the months, but by spring, it was seemingly complete. His world was bounded by four creviced walls and what they held. His spirit sat hunched within him, like an ancient stone man in these old stone walls, waiting without hope, he did not know for what: release into death or into life again, and until that time, crouched waiting, holding its strength gathered tight into itself, unobserved, seemingly forgotten.

XVI

THE REMOVAL

Cressy, at the London house, waited as usual for her husband's return. In the not quite three months since they had returned to it and it had become her only home, she had learned how to wait. She had learned how not to alarm herself with vague fears about his safety or her own; she had learned how not to be overwhelmed by torturing pictures of him finding pleasure in other houses and other beds, which was a hard lesson; she had learned how not to be pricked by jealous thoughts of his gay evenings with his friends where she was never asked to come. She could school herself now to present an equal spirit before the servants, as though she accepted and approved his habits, hoping they might somehow think she was at the center of his life, despite his open indifference.

This time, she thought, would be the same as any other. He

would be gone a week, two weeks, perhaps a month. He would stay longer than he thought, become involved. She might not even know the exact moment of his return, for she might be asleep, and he might set out again. She could not hold her attention on a book, and she felt too heavy to walk outside. The motion of the carriage made her ill. As the days lengthened, her mood varied between panic and lethargy. She went for walks and came back soon. She tried to read, and threw her novel down. She longed bitterly to share the hours with anyone. She did not see her father for almost a fortnight. He came by briefly one morning, and left his card, for she was still asleep. Another time he took her driving and tried to brighten her spirits. They neither one talked of the subject in their minds, her absent husband. She caught him looking at her attentively—"almost like a doctor," she thought—but so many thoughts and facts they would not either one speak of lay between them that they both found conversation difficult.

It was Robertson who brought matters to a head. He was deeply worried. She could not deceive him, and he perceived her distress, in which anger and anxiety and impatience mixed. Except for that strange period in the summer, he was not used to being left for so long a time, and he frankly did not believe it in the Marquis' nature to do it. He considered dispassionately that a woman might be involved, but he could not see that keeping the Marquis this length, and with no word from him. He worried more even than Cressy, but for a while he did not let her know it, because he disliked her and regarded her as the root of all their troubles.

After the Marquis had been gone a fortnight, Cressy went one morning and knocked at his bedroom door, as she had done several times, and paused, hoping that suddenly she would hear his voice answering. But she heard no sound, and she turned the door handle, which was now unlocked, and went slowly in. She had not been in his room before, and she looked about her, curiously. She was startled by a sound, beyond the dressing room door, and her hand flew to her mouth. Robertson came out at once, as startled as she, and looked at her angrily. She knew that he was thinking she had no business to be in this room, but nevertheless, she held her ground and looked back at him nervously. For a few seconds, neither spoke.

Then the valet said to her flatly: "This isn't right, my lady; his lordship should be back by now, or have sent a letter to us if he was delayed."

"You think he has been hurt? Fallen ill, or had an accident?" she asked faintly.

"I don't know what I think, but it's not like his lordship to leave us wondering like this."

She thought it very like him, but she did not say so.

"His lordship would send to us, unless some way he cannot," the valet said, "and I am very worried about it, but I don't know what to do. And I have no authority. But you have, my lady," he added accusingly.

She flushed. "What can I do? He would be so angry if I interfered."

"I would not think you would be thinking of such feelings, my lady, or let them stop you, when his lordship may be ill in some unequipped farmhouse, with a fever, or a broken leg from an overturned curricle."

"I do not think he would overturn his curricle, Robertson. I know he drives very fast, but he is very skilful."

"Wheels can come off," was all Robertson replied.

She looked at him helplessly. "What shall I do?"

He looked back at her, with less dislike, and said consideringly: "You might start by sending me out and let me make some enquiries. Where in the North did this Uncle live?"

She said blankly: "I don't know. He didn't tell me."

The valet masked his contempt, and said: "Someone must know, my lady. I'll see what I can do to find it out."

"His chaise is most distinctive. Someone surely will have seen it at some post house?"

"My lady, if we don't know the road he took, we won't know where to begin to ask. And he did not take his own equipage; it's still in the stables."

"That's strange," she said wonderingly, with a cold little fear she could not explain squeezing her heart. She could not recall the coach in which he left; her eyes had been full of tears, and her attention distracted.

"I thought so," the valet said, "when I learned it."

"It is not like him?"

The valet shook his head. "No, my lady, it is not."

"Perhaps it was more convenient for him on this trip? He might have thought his horses would be ill-stabled at his Uncle's, with things in confusion there?" It was too much for her, and she felt she was going to faint. He saw her go white, and put out his hand to steady her.

"Where's your vinaigrette, my lady?" he asked. She shook her head, unable to think or speak. "I'll go find a hartshorn, somewhere. Put your feet up, and lie your head down, like this, low."

She thought he seemed experienced in dealing with fainting ladies, and suddenly very like his master. She lay there wondering what she would do if the Marquis did not return. She had not before considered that he might not. He had always behaved so incomprehensibly, and of late had become so strange, to her this behaviour seemed no stranger than the rest. She did not have the visions of disaster his valet had. If he had gone, she privately believed that he had left because she bored him and her father annoyed him, and that the notion had taken him, once he had gone at all, to go permanently. She said as much to Robertson, on his return, in their new intimacy, but he pooh-poohed the notion.

"His lordship would not. His father was a gentleman. Perhaps his grandfather may have sometimes conducted himself in unusual ways, but his lordship is a gentleman, and he would not abandon a woman in, begging your ladyship's pardon, your ladyship's condition. Furthermore, he is attached to his horses, and to this house."

She smiled wistfully at this view of a man whom, inexplicably and irrationally, she loved but in whom she had found very little of what she called the gentleman. But if Robertson's view were at all the correct one, with only herself the exception, then she had been conducting herself in the manner of a silly green girl, indulging in attacks of vapours, preoccupied with her self-induced megrims, while her very real husband, for he was still that, stood in difficulties with no one to assist him. She determined to collect herself, and behave more suitably. She sent Robertson out employed to make all possible enquiries, and she herself took herself to look about the house with the eye of its mistress, not a visitor in it. She found much to embarrass her and to make herself ashamed, for the servants with no one to tax them had fallen into lazy habits; and although she might have found excuses for herself, she made none.

The next afternoon Cressy sat lingering over her tea that had been brought to her where she rested with her feet up on the chaise longue. She was very weary from her unaccustomed activities but in better spirits. She had decided that she must see that the house remained in its former good order. Should the Marquis return, in his own time, or should his valet find him ill or injured, he should not return, she determined, to a house in disorder and an afflicted wife, as he had left them, but to the place as he had known it before she came into it. "I have not assumed my responsibilities," she thought, "though I know very well how to do them; and even if it is at his own instructions that I stood idle, I am to blame in having followed them too closely and in having most unwisely too much feared to incur his displeasure." At a distance the Marquis seemed less formidable. But if he had not returned by the beginning of the Christmas season, which was hard upon them, she resolved to shut the London house and journey to the Duke of Adversane's country seat for the holidays, and for her child to be born there, in the New Year.

She sat down at the Marquis' desk, and found pen and paper there, and addressed herself to the task of writing the Marquis' father. She found it hard to explain why she had waited so long to acquaint the Duke with the fact of his son's disappearance, for fact she now perceived it to be, and not just a piece of devilry to torment her. She leaned back, thinking. She realised that with a man of her husband's sophistication and well-set habits, and his pride that he felt injured before his friends, her best efforts might have come to the same end. Although the marriage had been as unwelcome to herself as to him, nevertheless she had to admit that, however unwillingly, she had still agreed to it. But she had behaved herself more like a sulky, expectant girl, than the Marchioness of Gore. She had not given her attention to his needs or to his expectations. If he had not helped her or encouraged her, and in fact she knew well that he had not, she suddenly felt that her vulnerableness had led her to exaggerate his discourtesies, until they became in fact what at first she had only thought them to be. And he was very young himself, she thought, and despite his assured manner, might himself have been embarrassed by his return to London with an awkward, increasing wife.

She put her self-reproaches aside, and set herself again to finish her letter. She remembered suddenly very clearly what she had forgotten in the last unhappy fortnight, the Marquis' unusual sweetness to her at their parting. She wondered at it now, but she could find no meaning in it that made sense to her. A rush of longing swept over her, for all she briefly had and somehow lost, and never really had at all. She would have liked to put her head on his desk and weep her aching heart away, but instead she folded her letter and called the footman to see that it was posted. An unexpected thought came to her, that the Marquis might not have told his parents about her pregnancy, and so she wrote another letter to the Marquis' mother, informing her of it, and asking for her help.

If the Marquis' father was distressed at the news of her letter, and the discovery in it of a brother suddenly deceased and hitherto unknown to him, he concealed his feelings from her, and sent Cressy warm assurances of her welcome by himself and his wife at their home. Privately he wrote to have runners sent out to all points. His wife, concealing her surprise, wrote in delighted terms at the prospects of a grandchild and urged her to come sooner than Cressy had suggested, but Cressy did not change her plans. She had decided she must go through the Marquis' papers. She had found the names of his agent and his lawyer, and she had written to them, telling them of the Marquis' prolonged absence and asking if there were details she could see to, or needed to be told of. She had consulted the London doctor again, but she felt the Marquis' mother would know how to help her prepare best for the child's coming.

Robertson had returned, finally, with nothing at all to report. He was disturbed, not only about his master's health, but what should happen to himself. She prevailed upon him, with no great difficulty, to add himself at her request, temporarily to the Duke of Adversane's service. She would herself be lost, she felt, without him now, and told him so. Robertson had thought she would return to her father's house, in the Marquis' absence, and he was surprised and gratified to hear her plans, and looked at her with more affection.

Her father was disappointed she did not intend to come for Christmas at Rotherby, and he hoped yet to change her mind. He spoke to her of the plans he had for the festivities, but her family seemed more alien to her at this time, some way, than strangers, and she held no festive humour. She knew how little her father liked her husband, and she felt she could not have Gore find her there, even though he had himself suggested such a visit. The birth daily grew more imminent, and she wanted his child to be born where he himself was born, among his things, surrounded by the people who knew him and would love his child for his sake, not for hers. Her instincts for her infant had grown strong in her, and knowing her father's arbitrary ways, and wishing to avoid arguments, she set ahead her departure by several days. She did not entirely close the Marquis' house but left a staff of servants there, taking only her abigail and his valet and the coachman with her. Her father, arriving the next morning determined to bring her to his home, found an empty house.

XVII

THE SEVENTH INTERLUDE

THE LYING-IN

Christmas that year was not a joyous time. The Marquis' absence, still unexplained, overclouded it. And yet the days had their contentments. The Marquis' parents had welcomed their guest because she was their son's wife and great with child, but after she had been there for several days, they welcomed her for her own sake.

They had been surprised when the Marquis had brought her home as his wife because although they knew her slightly and approved of what they knew, she was not the type of girl they had expected to appeal to their reckless son. In fact, she was not like the type that had already appealed, and they had had serious misgivings, which they kept to themselves, about her future happiness with him. They had been even more surprised at the quiet manner of their courting and the sudden abruptness of their marriage. Had they lived more in London and been more worldly, they might have wondered more. Living quietly, they simply accepted it, though they did not understand, without questioning the oddness. Now, becoming acquainted with their daughter-in-law, they found her very much after their own heart.

She pleased them all with her modesty and her quiet wit, and they thought her very brave to be so near her time and still so casual. It was a casualness born of innocence and despair. She had learned in a thorough school the nature of necessity: that what is truly inexorable must be gone through with, as quietly and as well as possible, and with as little fuss. But they saw only a small, brave girl with a quick smile and withdrawn eyes, who though she did not speak very much herself, wanted to listen to all they had to say.

The Duke showed her his books and took her around the estate, its avenue, its woods, its linden trees and oaks, its rush-filled ponds and bridges, where the Marquis liked to shoot, its high meadows bare now of the hay, even the enclosed garden where the Marquis' and his family's pets lay buried, while she searched his face for a resemblance which she did not at first find. The Duchess took her through the house and showed her family portraits, and when she could pull her daughter-in-law away, through the still-room and the buttery and the gardens near the house and the sundial in the dormant rose garden and the little stone frog on a lily pad hidden near a bench that the Marquis as a child had loved. Without meaning to, they told her more than they intended, about the Marquis' education and their differences, as he grew older. She listened to all their stories, hungrily. She listened to his father tell about his ways with horses before his head reached the bottom of the stirrup, his fearlessness, his youthful scholarship that amazed the Vicar until he actually translated what it meant, his ingenious adventures, and some that went beyond mere mischief, his need for discipline, the frequent discipline he got, his generosities, and his growing reticences, after he went away to school. She listened to his mother: the stories of his babyhood, his boyhood, his wild ways that so exasperated and so perplexed his gentle father, but not herself, because, she said, she well remembered her own so different father who had baffled everyone. And for all that, so loving and so affectionate, his mother said, even Adversane could not be angry with him long.

Cressy built a different picture of the Marquis from these stories in her mind, and set it against her own brief memories of him, first as a young boy and then as a man, and tried to reconcile the two, his family's and her own. She would often go away by herself and sit before the pictures of him and the other Adversanes. She especially liked one of him as a boy of ten, erect, his laughing eyes filled with his youthful courage and high spirits, painted out-of-doors, the wind and sun upon him, his horse behind him. Just so she had seen him once. But the pictures, though she could trace in them the features now familiar to her, seemed in a way to be of another person, for they were flat and still and did not move. She would shut her eyes then, and let her own memories slip through behind her eyes. She somehow could not believe that he was dead, and all her knowledge to lie useless. "But then," she thought, "there will be his son" (a son, somehow, she always thought), "and I must know these things to tell him—at least."

On Christmas Day, the Duchess brought down the cradle she had used for the Marquis when he was an infant, and gave it to Cressy for her own. She looked at the cradle, and she could not believe that her tall, agile husband, with his steely strength, had once fit into so compact a space and lain helpless there.

She expressed as much to the Duchess: "Bysshe slept in that? I do not believe it!"

The Duchess laughed, and said, conceding: "Well, he did not stay that way very long, even as an infant."

She was shown his coral and his bells and his papspoon, and she sighed at the brief vision of a world she was to enter in, which she could not imagine. For the first time, though, she found her husband endearing, and even funny.

Both her father and her brothers came on Christmas Day with gifts, and her father came to see her after that several times, alone. He saw that she was sad, beneath her smiles, but he laid it to the nearness of her time, and he privately cursed the Marquis for bringing her to it. It did not occur to him that she missed her husband and grieved for him. He had to be content to see her there, for though she talked lovingly with him, he felt a slight constraint, and she would not leave Adversane's estate. She felt she could not bear to see her father's house, or to be in it, with the memories she had there.

There had not been snow for Christmas, but after Christmas the cold set in, and it snowed steadily for two weeks. The Duke of Adversane engaged a midwife and a nurse to live in their house, in case the doctor could not reach them. It was snowing when her labours began. Robertson was despatched to bring the doctor, who found her docile and unafraid. This birth, she knew, was the ending of a story for her, and the beginning of another; what the second might be she could not foresee, but as part of that first story, she gave herself to it and its discomforts yieldingly. She had known such fear and humilation at the child's conceiving that the fear and humiliations of its birth seemed a little thing to her, and she grew urgent to see its face at last, and bent all her efforts to help it in its release. "I shall break," she thought, and then she cried: "Oh, Bysshe, it is too much!" She felt a last sharp pain and then she felt the child slide from her. She lay there, peacefully again, listening to the doctor and the midwife move about her and the room, ministering to herself and to the infant. She heard the baby give a furious cry, and saw its slippery limbs, and then they laid it, warm and heavy, on her.

"You have a boy, my lady," the doctor said, smiling down at her. "You did very well, you should be proud. It is a fine baby, and very like his father, when I delivered him."

She studied its features carefully when they brought it to her first to nurse, after it had fed and fallen asleep. She looked at the smooth veined eyelids like little shells, the long eyelashes resting on the cheeks, the smiling, relaxed, now happy mouth, the tiny ears lying flat against the skull, the faintly traced arches of the eyebrows in shape so dear to her, the downy powdering of dark hair.

"It is beautiful," she said happily. "But does it look like his son?" she added doubtfully.

"It does indeed," the Marquis' father said. "I remember well." He added with satisfaction: "And he has the family head, it's unmistakable."

"They all do," the Marquis' mother said. "Haven't you noticed? Bysshe's father does," and she showed her what they meant. "It has just his look," she added. "You know Bysshe's eyes—he looks at you and laughs, and you forgive him anything. They are closed now, but I can tell." The Duchess was amused, but Cressy felt an inward pain. Did she indeed not know—

"To me he is too little to tell," Cressy said. "I never saw a person so small as this."

" 'He is little, but he will grow,' " the Marquis' father said reminiscently. "We tire you, Cressy, we will come another time."

The days changed now for Cressy. Her nature's bent was to be happy, and it would have been a sour heart that did not rejoice with such a babe, she thought. She held him to her breast, caressingly, as she could not his father, and lay back contented, shut in the timeless rhythmic world that encloses the mother and her suckling child. She did not forget her husband; he was part of herself now. She thought of him almost all the time, as naturally as she breathed, and his dear face she saw before her, each day more clearly, shadowed in the tiny features of their child. But the days slipped into weeks and months, winter into spring and into summer, as she cared for her child and watched him grow. She did not want to name him without the Marquis' advice, but the matter pressed her, so she gave him the names of the Marquis' father and of hers.

That gentleman, her father, remarked a report published in July in his journal that gave him cause for concern. He sent to Paris for more news, without success, and for weeks, waited in a concealed state of curiosity, not unmixed with fear. At that time he never went out alone, or without his pistols. But as the months of July and then August drew to a close, he breathed more easily, and relaxed, and in the end, without mixed feelings, considered the matter of the Marquis finally closed. He became a frequent visitor at his grandson's side, remarking the clear likeness with satisfaction—although a child looking like a butcher's baby would not have shaken his conviction or made him feel remorse.

After his grandson's first birthday, the Duke of Salisbury privately urged upon his daughter to accept invitations and go out again into society. The unsavoury and near scandalous episode with the Marquis finished (although he could not explain to her his reasons for believing that the Marquis was dead), he had hopes that she would leave her widowed state and live a happier life. In this, he was neither encouraged nor discouraged by the sympathetic Duke of Adversane, who also believed his son must be dead. But Cressy, though she smiled and listened politely, neither put on widow's weeds, nor went into society. She rode with her brothers, took an interest in the Duke's estate and in her Grace's house, was daughterly to her father, and kept her own counsel. The tiny new Marquis learned to walk, and to know his grandfathers, his grandmother, his two amusing uncles who were so hard for him to tell apart, and to speak, and did not know that he lacked anything.

XVIII

THE REBIRTH

On a summer's day the history of the Marquis and the history of a time and place met and briefly touched each other. To the Marquis, listlessly hunched in his stone room, the day began as any other, but when it ended, his eight months' imprisonment had also ended, violently bursting him not only back to life and into life, but into the brilliance of the July sun.

At the first, the noises that he heard seemed to him like the heavy, far-off echoes of noises of any day, but on this particular day they did not fade away, as on other days, but grew and crescendoed until they ceased to be echoes of noise, and once again he was surrounded by sound. It was deafeningly loud, painful on his ears half-deafened by unuse. He put his hands over his ears to shut out the noise and lessen the pain piercing his eardrums, and though he did not know it, cowered like an animal, in a corner of his cave-like room. If he thought at all, he thought he would be destroyed in the rampaging destruction that seemed imminently to be about to pull the fortress over and bury him beneath. It was in this way that they found him, when they battered at and finally unlocked his indestructible door. They took him by the hands and pulled him, crouching and panic-stricken, out of his cell. They would have ridden him on their shoulders, in triumph, but he screamed and bit in terror, and his staring vacant eyes and long filthy matted elflocks repulsed them in turn. They dropped him, and he scuttled off behind a pillar, and watched them furtively.

After a bit, seeing that no one paid him any mind, any more, his ears throbbing and aching, uncomprehending what had happened but realising just so much that the doors were all unlocked and that he might, mixing with the rout, walk where they walked, he walked hesitantly down the long halls and corridors and up the stairs, out of the great doors into the sunlight, his own man again. The sunlight pierced and blinded his eyes, as the noise had his ears, and he flung his arm over them and shut them, the lids flaming red even though shut. He turned away from the sun, back against the doors which had opened to receive him, and now had opened to eject him. He did not question the miracle, he only wanted it to continue long enough to allow him to be somewhere else before it ended.

He did not look so very different from many of the ragged, dirty wild-haired citizens of the street, and he quietly disengaged himself from their interest by threading his way in and out of them, now hiding, now moving, until he was only one among a great crowd. He walked and continued walking, without direction, until he came to an immense stone church. It promised quiet and dimness of light and loneliness, his companions for so many days that he could not relinquish them easily. He stumbled in and crouched in a corner, and huddled there, how long he never knew. In fact, this part of his release was already fading from his mind, and as it faded, a remnant of his old self returned to him.

He realised he was crouching in a corner of the vestibule, and he stood up and straightened himself, and holding himself rather painfully erect, walked into the church. But there was nowhere there to sit, and so he walked out again, his unused legs wanting to fold under him, and found a kind of bench, near another door, and sat there, for a long time not thinking. The minutes slipped by, and lengthened into hours, and he began to be hungry and realised that he had no money at all and that no one would feed him or help him. With an instinct he realised he must leave the city, with its mobs of ragged hungry people, like himself, and somehow find his way into the country. He set his face in one direction, away from the sun, and began to walk.

He did not afterwards remember how long or how far he walked, or how he managed to continue, but all the time being governed by his instincts more than by his conscious reasons, his instincts telling him that he must walk to survive, walk he did. His imprisonment, comparatively short, had not crippled him—his faculties or his muscles—only subjected them to a temporary paralysis, and now, in the warmth of the day, and the width of the world open again to him, it began slowly, somewhat, to leave.

On the way he took a crust of bread from a child, and a piece of bone from a dog, and his water from the troughs kept for the horses, and these sustained his march. When night came, he stopped and fell asleep where he was. When the sun rose, he continued in the same direction. Eventually the city ended, as his instinct told him it must, but the parts he walked through did not enter into his eyes or remain in his mind. The green meadows and the green trees rose up around him and the fields of wheat laced with poppies and cornflowers and daisies. He looked at them unbelieving and continued his walk. When he passed a house, he went in for help, but he went in many without finding it. The things he had found to eat on his walk, raw fruits and vegetables and grains, his stomach and his bowels had been unable to accept and he became ill and further weakened with retching and dysentery. But it was not until some ten miles further that the kindness of the country reasserted itself, and he found a farmer who took pity on him and took him in for a hired labourer.

It would be true in its way to say that he did not remember who he had been. He did not wish to remember, he wanted only quiet and forgetfulness and the peace they gave. During the day he worked, though for some time he was of little use. For the rest, he ate and slept, and put all his past behind him, remembering nothing before the moment when they took him in, ill and starving, fed him thin gruel, and put him into a bed. He had stayed there for several days, he did not know how many, and the farmer and his wife were too kind to tell him, when finally he woke with a clear head, and a stomach free of gripe. He made his way out of the bed, and staggered into the kitchen where he found the farmer and his wife, who looked curiously at their labouring guest.

"I have been ill," he said. "I do not know who I am or how I have come here, or where I have been. But perhaps if you will help me to a bath, and a comb, I can find out more when I see what I look like." But when he was bathed, with the help of the farmer's sons, and the rats' nests and tangles and the creatures in his hair washed and combed out, and the long strands tied back with a string, and a smock and breeches loaned him, and sabots, in place of his torn coat and shirt, filthy beyond recognition of colour or material, and his broken boots, he did not recognise himself at all, so he was no further along. He did not tell them he was English, but used their language altogether. Having gone to ground, he had the instinct to stay there until his torn nerves healed and his torn self should become whole.

So he stayed, all through the summer months. He fished for them, planted for them, weeded for them, trundled compost and manure, picked fruit, reaped hay, winnowed chaff, drove sheep and cows, each day having its tasks and its rest. He found it infinitely soothing, and he began as the summer changed into autumn to walk again with some vigour in his step, and to hold his head easily erect. He could walk faster and ride farther and work harder and longer and not tire, as the days passed, and he took delight in his returning strength and abilities. The farmer had six children. Three older boys, old enough to help, two little girls just learning to help their mother, and to take care of the youngest child, a very small boy. A restful family, he thought. He was relieved, without asking himself why, that the daughters should be so small. The life there was not touched by the life of Paris, with its violence, nor by the life of any other place except itself.

When fall came, and the golden leaves had blown from the

trees, he found his memory had imperceptibly been returning until, with no conscious single moment of return, he knew very well who he was, and where he had lived, and that he had a wife, and parents, and responsibilities. But he made no move to reach them or to return to them. He had no idea how he could, even if he wished to, but he did not wish. He looked down at his long hands and fingers, growing calloused and hard and brown, and he was amused. If his family had worried about him once, nearly a year ago, he did not imagine that they still did. He could not imagine them caring, for he did not. His emotions to all that he had left behind, never strong, were as dead now as the November leaves. His thought whistled through his dry brain to as little effect as the November wind, and his heart towards his wife, only just stirring when he was abruptly rapt from her, was wholly withered and dormant. He knew, of course, that the cycle of nature was dormancy and then a re-springing, but being a man, and not a plant, he did not foresee it for himself. To think of them tired him, and so he thought of them as little as possible.

The season of the grape was upon them, then the season of the pig. He gave himself up wholeheartedly to the changes of the seasons and the duties each brought, with the zest of the unfamiliar, not knowing that if one gives oneself wholeheartedly to one thing, one may yet do it for another. He had never been a man to relish the natural world: it had been an obstacle, or a place, to get through from the room of one house into another, or a playground in which to hunt or walk or court. But here under the wintry skies, barren, stripped, he came to follow its moods both for the profit to the farm and for its own sake. He enjoyed the lack of any special time or place, of not being bound by his society, its customs, its dress, its manners, its whims. For the first time that he could remember, he felt a free man. He had been a libertine, and made himself free of people and places and of his society and even of the girl who was his wife, but he could not remember being free both in himself and of himself before. He took great joy in it, the more because without admitting it he nevertheless knew that no man, particularly not himself, could long remain so free.

The anniversary of his imprisonment came and went, with no special bitterness on his part, and only a casual remembrance when the first snows fell. He did not wish to think back, for pain lay that way, and he could not yet bear pain again. His abhorrence of it, and the involved ways in which he sought to avoid the most casual pain, surprised him, but even as it surprised him, he forgot it. The snows came, and the land lay white and smooth and glistening under the moon. Like the flesh of the earth, or its innocence, he thought. Sounds were muted, work was less. The family began thinking of Père Noël, and making preparations. He enjoyed the children, watching them play, and fight, and play again, alone or with each other, or with their parents. Sometimes he played with them. It was a world he had not known of and never dreamed of. But he never thought of his own child, or wondered whether it had lived, or what its sex was.

He enjoyed watching the farmer Jean and his wife Marie, who unlike himself now lived very much within their own time and place and century and society, what there was of that. Their world was bound so rigidly by necessity—of days and nights each with its required times and tasks, of seasons, and the needs of their animals and their children and their plantings—that they seemed to him innocent of the evil of boredom. He supposed that they had sins; he imagined their priest, whom he had met, would say so, but he found none in them himself. He enjoyed their scoldings of one another, and their warm, unspoken affections, and at night he enjoyed, without envy, hearing them from time to time turn one another in their bed. He supposed they did not know he heard, but he imagined they would not have cared much, had they known. What he did not know was that he himself was a continual source of interest and amusement to them all, like a strange visitor from another world, as indeed he was.

When the last snows began to fall, or not to fall, and the fields began to emerge dripping and brown from their winter's cover, he felt bereft. The winter had sheltered him, and he hated the inexorable coming of the spring, with its movement and its stir and its selfish preoccupations with renewal. He would have held it back if he could. He fought against its insinuous advances, its warmth, its opening scents and colours. But he could not hold it back, inexorable, invading. It banished the winter, despite the winter's final forays and rushes, and invaded even him. Once they were there, not even his crabby spirit could resist the trembling flowering trees, the green shoots of grain and wheat and flowering bulbs. And everything he saw put Cressy into his mind. He saw her whole and he saw her in part everywhere he looked and everywhere he went. Like the spring, the memory of her invaded him, and like the merciless spring, he could not push her out. He did not want her, he did not wish to go back, he wanted only to stay where he was, happy and oblivious. But the leaves pushed themselves up and out and surrounded the trees, and his memories pushed all about him, in him, through him, utterly surrounding and engulfing him.

As the spring moved on, as springs always have and will, the little lambs and kids were born, and everywhere he looked, he saw a calf or foal or chick standing with its mother, butting at her, nursing her, galloping wildly about her. Even the farmer's wife Marie was rounding out again, warm and summery in her good nature. His thoughts turned of themselves to his own little lamb, and he found himself wondering about it and about its mother. Finally, in July, he wrote to her. Even after he had come to the decision, which in the end seemed to make itself, it had taken him some weeks to come by adequate material on which and with which to send his message. He wrote, his unaccustomed pen bare and stripped of grace, travelling labouriously and slowly:

Wife,
  I am here on Jean Laurentier's farm not far from St. Denis. I would like to come home, but I have no money, and the country is unsettled. Will you send me what you will by my former valet Robertson, if he can be found to do it? I cannot tell you now how I am here, or why you have not heard from me. My love to you and to the child.
                              Gore

He dated the letter, and sent it to her at his London house, hoping that it would somehow find her and that she would accept it and pay the postage.

XIX

THE RECOVERY

The letter reached Cressida, delayed by the Paris disorders, finally in August. It had gone first as he directed to the London house that was shut, and then had been sent down to her at his father's house, where she now stayed. They liked to have her and their son's child, and she felt most a sense of belonging when she was there, though she did not wish to probe her reasons why. She was alone when the letter was brought to her. She did not know whether after so long she had ceased hoping to hear from him, but when she saw the letter, with the foreign postmark and the unknown hand, she felt sick with an apprehension that quickly changed to a puzzled joy. She had never had a letter from him before, and so she had no way of knowing how his letters were, but this brief note, with so much unsaid, unasked, seemed somehow most strange to her.

She took it to his mother, who said straightway: "This is not Gore's hand." Then the Duchess looked at it more closely: "Perhaps it might be, if he were hurt or had been ill. But if he has been sick, I do not see why he should not just say so. And I do not find his signet. Maybe it is a French trap? It does not sound like Bysshe at all. And he doesn't even ask you if you will take him back, after all these months without a word, he seems to just assume it."

"If he does, indeed he is right to, and that is very like him, to assume," Cressy said. "But look, Belle-maman, he has addressed the letter to me, not to you or to his father. He knows if I am very angry with him, too angry to be just and give his message, I can throw away his letter and no one will ever know about it. And it is not Robertson who will find the moneys." She stayed a moment, thinking. "It is not Robertson who should go, I think. I shall go myself, if Beau-père will take me."

"What of your own father, Cressy, or your strong young brothers?"

"They do not always get along," Cressy said briefly. "I'd rather go with someone of his own." She did not say aloud, "someone I can trust to help him, not to harm him." The suspicions that lay behind her mind she had not made plain even to herself.

"His father does not always get along with him either, my dear."

"Then I shall go with Robertson, I think."

"That is not sufficient, Cressy."

"I am a matron, Belle-maman," Cressy said. "But if you wish, then I shall go with Robertson and Beau-père too, if he will go. Will you keep the babe for me?"

But she could not set out at once. There were dispositions and instructions to make concerning the child. A trip had to be made to Gore's bank, and also considerable enquiry about the safety of travel through France, about which they could get no certain information, although the disturbances in Paris for the moment seemed less. It was the first of September before they finally set off in coach and four. She had been unusually secretive, and without explaining, she had made Gore's mother promise to tell no one about the letter, and also his father. On the trip to Gore's father, she explained nothing at all to Robertson except for her wish for his assistance, and she had packed a change of clothes for her husband with her own, herself. She giggled slightly as she did it, thinking of his valet's shock if he had known the desecrations she made on his clothes. But she was seriously concerned, why she could not say, that no one else at all should know of the reasons for the trip or the direction they planned to go. She let Gore's parents lay it to her girlish nervousness; what they thought did not matter, so long as they did not break her secret. Also, her longing was so intense, she was afraid to name it to anyone, or to hope that they would really find him, after all these months, himself and safe.

She sat wrapped in seeming meditation on the journey in the chaise, and on Gore's yacht across the Channel, but she was not thinking. She held herself empty, like a vase, waiting to learn what in the end she must think. They avoided the city Paris, and made directly for the little village to the North that Gore had named. There they put into the Inn, and made enquiries about the farm of one Jean Laurentier. It did not appear that it would be hard to find. She forgot how many days and weeks had passed since the letter had been written and sent, and she did not conceive that waiting, with no answer, as day passed into day, Gore would finally have dismissed hope.

And he had hoped. Once the letter had gone, he had suddenly wanted very much to go home. But he could not go without money. He shrank from the prospect, or from the idea of going back if he was not wanted. But he wanted to go. As August passed, and he heard nothing, and Robertson did not appear, he schooled himself to accept disappointment. He had treated his wife badly, and made nothing of her needs and wishes. He had meant to give her a chance to deny him his, as he had hers, but still he hoped irrationally she would not.

The wheat was ready to be harvested, and he was standing in it with the farmer and his sons, with their sickles sharpened and ready. The wife and little girls were waiting behind them with the straws to bind the handfuls into sheaves. Underfoot the blue cornflowers and the scarlet poppies gleamed even when their heads were trampled low. It was this group that Cressy saw. The Duke of Adversane had gone towards the farmhouse to make enquiries, when she saw the men in the field, and on impulse, directed the coachman to drive a little forward. Dismounting from the coach, she left the valet behind, at her urgent request, while she went to make enquiries of her own of the farmers. She did not see anyone like her husband, and she could not bear a disappointment now in front of Robertson or the Duke, or any longer waiting. She did not at all imagine one of the reapers to be the Marquis, and so she approached unsuspicioning.

But he saw her. First the strange coach, and as his hopes leaped, his heart leaped too as he saw her descend and recognised her. She was wearing a light straw bonnet against the sun, tied beneath her chin, and her dress, though made for travelling, was in the latest style. Here, into his brief world outside of time, time came invading. He was very aware of his unpowdered hair, loosely tied, escaping in the heat, and his sweaty smock. But not embarrassed, rather much amused, picturing her astonishment. But thank God, he thought, she didn't send Robertson. It would be too much for the poor fellow to have to endure the sight. He wondered briefly if she had come alone, but his emotions were too intense to allow him to dwell on what that might entail.

For a moment, he considered turning away, to tease her, prolonging the masquerade and delaying the sharp moment, but he dared not risk teasing his fate. He might turn and she would not be there. His anticipation seemed to rise and choke him, but it was not visible. She only saw a tall young farmer, sickle in hand, standing there in the ripe wheat, waiting, watching her approach. He stood there, gravely, waiting to see the moment when she knew him. But he did not see it. She had so long schooled herself to hide her feelings from him and from the world, that when she knew him, her face did not change, nor her step. She walked straight to him, and held out her hands to him to take, and then she smiled, into his surprised and delighted eyes. He took them, and bent his head and kissed them both, and then gently, so that she might stop him if she wished, before he soiled her dress, he pulled her, hands and all, into the circle of his arms against his smock. He did not say a word, not even her name, nor did she, but they stood there so long, that the other reapers paused to watch, and his father, returned, and his valet in the coach grew impatient and came out to greet them, knowing now quite well who stood there in the field.

The two men's faces were both comical mixtures of stern disapproval, and profound relief and happiness. They both felt that the Marquis had behaved unspeakably, unforgivably, in leaving his wife near her time, and sending no word to her or to anyone. They found that hard to forgive. But they felt no need to wonder if they could forgive it, they were so over-whelmed to find him again, alive and well. For in the midst of their disapproval had always been the fear that he did not, only because he could not. His father's interest also glanced on the golden corn in which they stood, with the particular inter-est of the landholder, and he had picked a bearded head, as he came, which nodded in his fingers. Robertson's delight was tempered by perceiving the costume (he could only call it that) in which his master stood, without self-consciousness or embarrassment. He arrived across the field in a walking state of shock, that deepened as his practised eye took in the whole from wooden shoes to unkempt hair.

"Not knowing what we meant to do, her ladyship's not hav-ing informed me," he said reproachfully, "I have not brought your lordship's clothes with me."

"I have," Cressy said, looking him over, "if they still fit you. You seem much larger, though perhaps what you have on just makes you look so."

"I may well be. I shall probably have to have new coats made—all of them," he said, smiling at her, his voice choking on the laughter in his throat. She smiled back at him happily. They began to walk slowly back towards the farmhouse, the other reapers converging on them.

Cressy treated his being met in a smock in a French wheat-field, almost two years after his disappearance, as if it were the most natural and expected event. She did not seem to want him to explain, or to speak of whatever had been prior to the meeting, and with some surprise and some gratitude, he followed the lead she gave him. There was really very little to delay them at the house. His Grace was anxious to begin the return journey, for though the land was peaceful here, he found the reports from Paris terrible and terrifying. The labourer having been worthy of his hire, but possessing nothing, only the changing of his clothes delayed them. They did not fit so well, as before, but well enough that his new presence cast a sudden constraint on the members of the family with whom he had lived so contentedly these many months. He looked at them with much affection, and bent down and kissed the children, and shook their hands. He even kissed his former master, and his wife, and was soundly embraced in return. His Grace the Duke looked on with amazement, and his valet who had been sent on to the chaise, was spared this shock. Cressy was touched by their fondness and their kind hearts. She went forward and thanked them for taking such care of her lord in his need. Both she and the Marquis' father proffered them separate gifts of money, and left them as thank offerings. But time pressed them, and they made their departure.

The Marquis, after they were at his father's chaise, stood still a minute longer, looking at the golden fields, and the far-off figures by the house. It had been just a little more than a year before that he had come this road, to this place, ill and fainting. He did not push the memory from him this time, but he stood there, remembering. One day, he thought, he would come back and stand here again and see these alien people, whose blood he partly shared, where he had learned lessons he had not known before about the simple needs and unaffected love that gratified them.

He winked at his valet above, and swung himself into the body of the travelling chaise and took his place beside his wife. He did not look forward to the conversation he knew must follow, in the privacy of the coach's moving room. How eventually he was going to deal with the situation he did not know, but he knew that he was not going to tell his wife about her father's part in it, because he did not want to hurt her; and he was not going to tell his father, because it was an end, if it were possible, to these hostilities he wanted, not a fresh beginning. And about his imprisonment and the release, the details of which they would most predictably and naturally be curious to learn more of, once they knew of it at all, he still simply did not want to think or talk.

When it began to appear that the Marquis had no intention of saying anything (he was leaning back comfortably, and smiling tenderly and rather foolishly into his wife's eyes, and she into his), the Duke of Adversane decided that if any sense was to come out of this strange affair, the opening must be initiated by himself. Accordingly, he began forbiddingly: "This is all very well, and we are glad to see you and to have found you; but I think, Bysshe, some explanation of your absence is due us."

"I haven't very much to give," the Marquis said apologetically. "One of my enemies—I have made many, sire—somehow procured a *lettre de cachet* and had me put away in France."

His father looked amazed. "That would be an uncommonly unfriendly enemy to put himself to so much trouble when a footpad would have done as well in London, and for less expense."

The Marquis did not answer him directly. He smiled faintly. "You do not believe me? I assure you that is exactly what occurred. I hardly believed it myself."

Cressy looked at him in horror, and he understood, he thought, her reason for it. Her words faltered: "My lord, is this true?"

"It must be, if I say it," he said gently. "Do not distress yourself, my lady; it is past now."

"Such a thing was done to you and you don't know by whom?" his father asked, incredulous.

The Marquis moved his head slightly. "I was set upon by several men unknown to me on my way from London. After I left you, Cressy," he said, turning to her. "It occurred to me then they might have been hired by friends of Teviot."

"Teviot? Why friends of his?" the Duke asked, astounded.

"I believe, sir, I had just shot him in a duel."

"I never heard of it," his father said in surprise, "and I have seen Teviot frequently."

"*Seen* Teviot?" asked the Marquis in greater surprise.

"In fact, in London just the fortnight last," continued Adversane. "He surely did not bear you that kind of grudge."

"I thought, sir, I had killed him," the Marquis said, having listened to this speech with feelings of the profoundest relief.

"You were overconfident, then," said his father. "The young are hard to kill, they have amazing elasticity." He looked at his son intently. "How is it you are here now? I had heard one does not leave such places. Did your enemy relent?"

The lines in the Marquis' face deepened and he shook his head, and he did not speak for several minutes. Then he said, with a forced lightness: "I believe there is some sort of Revolution presently here in France? I had cause—some months ago—to be grateful to its processes. In the midst of them I was allowed to leave unnoticed, and I came here, to the farm, where we have met."

"But that was last summer," the Duke said, again surprised, "if you mean the Paris fortress, I forget its name. Were you in there?"

"I believe so," said the Marquis absently.

His father opened his mouth to speak, then closed it tightly, as he observed his son's face. After a minute, he said, nevertheless sternly: "It is now a year past that time, and you never let us know. That was cruelly done, Bysshe. It has caused us great distress."

"I am sorry for it. I was not myself," the Marquis said simply. "Let us speak of other things now. It is past. I am glad to see your Grace, and you my wife." The tears were flowing down her cheeks, as she listened to him. She put her hand in his and pressed it and he held it tightly.

"You were imprisoned for, if I count correctly, eight months," the Duke said slowly. He stared at the Marquis with a thoughtful eye. "I have heard stories about it. Were you well-treated there?"

"In part," the Marquis said. "It was not very amusing. I don't recommend the place to you."

"I shall find the person and the ruffians who dared affront my son, and myself, in such a way!" Adversane declared stiffly, his face hard.

The Marquis felt his wife trembling beside him, and he wondered what she knew. "It was two years ago, sire, or nearly. I would not recognise the men again. They took care I should not see them." He felt her relaxing again beside him, and he added: "They might even have mistook me for some other victim and missed their aim."

"I do not see how," his Grace commented. "Your name would have to be on a *lettre de cachet*, and the person who procured it would have to be someone in a high place. It would be a strange error, for anyone to make."

"I do not know about that," the Marquis said indifferently. "My face is not well-known there. Error or not, it was some time ago. Let us speak of other things, of more importance." He turned to Cressy. "Am I the father of a daughter or a son?"

"A son, my lord," Cressy said with some wonderment.

"A son!" the Marquis exclaimed. "Oh, lord, I hope he's not like me! Would you not say so, my sire?"

The Duke, not a tactless man, perceived his son's reluctance and distress, beneath his lightness, and stopped his inquisition. Whatever his son's reasons, his own curiosity could wait. So he told the Marquis stories about his friends, and about his home, and Cressy told him stories about his son. The trip passed quietly and uneventfully and in comparative comfort. They stopped that night at an inn on the road, exhausted, the Marquis too tired to think of supper. There was considerable coming and going, and in the public rooms much revolutionary talk of politics, and the latest motions of the King. Cressy was frightened by the roughness, and they took their supper in their rooms. The Marquis fell asleep over it, and between them, they put him in his bed. The Marquis' father had with simple natural feeling engaged two rooms, one for himself and Robertson, and one for his son and his wife, not having known of their estrangement.

In the middle of the night the Marquis had bad dreams, and tossed and cried aloud in his sleep. Cressy woke beside him, and took his head in her lap, and rocked him and soothed him.

"What have I said?" he cried bewildered and distressed, waking.

"Nothing, my dear lord," she comforted him, "you were dreaming of another place, but you are here now, you are home."

"Home?" He looked still bewildered. "Have I a home? Where is it?"

"It is here, my dearest lord," she said, slipping beneath him, and clasping him lightly to her. "Will you come?"

He accepted her gratefully, and slept again, and in the morning he seemed to remember nothing. The next day and night passed in the same pattern. They travelled in easy stages all day, talking of casual matters, but at night he had violent distressing dreams, until she held and comforted him, and took him to her, distracted and hardly awake. She did not speak of it the next morning, nor did he, and she was not sure he knew, but she wondered about these dreams, what he had seen, what had been done to him, and how long he had had them, and how long they would go on. She could not know that their immediate source was the prospect of the encounter with her father.

The next day they were at the sea. Leaving the hired coach,

they embarked at once. The yacht was waiting where they had left it, the wind was fresh, and the tide at the full, ready. The Marquis' joy to see his own ship surprised them, and almost alarmed them by its unwonted intensity. His face was illuminated by it, like a flame. The voyage this time was rougher, and Cressy and his father both went below, but the Marquis stayed in the air on the upper deck. Nothing persuaded him to go below, not even to enquire about them. The salt wind blew through his hair, and the spray whipped his cheeks, and he strained forwards as though he could whip the ship forward, his eyes staring ahead for the first glimpse of the coast he had left without expectation of return.

XX

THE FINAL EPISODE

THE RESOLVING

The Marquis had thought they would be going to their London house, but the Marchioness told him she had closed it, so they went instead immediately to his Grace's seat in the country. "Where your mother waits for you," said the Duke. "And your son," said Cressy. After tea they met him. He came towards them, on his steady legs, a big boy now, of the estate of nearly two. He looked at his father fearlessly, cheerfully, from the safety of his mother, and his father looked at him, and saw his own hair and eyes, and features stamped on another's face, and marvelled that he could have ever thought it possible to disclaim such a true breeding, or wished to.

"What will he do, if I pick him up?" he whispered to Cressy.

"You must try and see; he is not very used to strangers," she said, "and he doesn't know you aren't one."

Seated on his lap, the baby looked at him gravely, but he did not cry.

"He will know you soon, my lord," Cressy promised, taking him. "But oh, my dear, how much you've missed of him. I shall have to tell it all to you."

"Why tell me?" he suggested, bending a look on her. "When we have more, I'll see it all again, for don't you think it will be much the same?"

"You are profane, my lord," she said blushing, "for they are not the same."

"But I daresay I'll find a certain likeness there," he replied, smiling down at her.

He took her hand, swinging it lightly back and forth, and walked with her and his son out into the garden. They sat down on a bench, beneath the late summer honeysuckle and the climbing roses, still in September, and watched their son chasing bugs, very peacefully.

"Has he found my frog?" asked the Marquis.

Her eyes sparkled, and she nodded. "By himself," she said, "though he had not you to show him."

"That's the best way," he said cheerfully. Then he sighed. "We shall have to go see your father soon." He paused and wryly smiled at her. "He doesn't like me, you know."

"No," she agreed.

"Well, if he's not pleased to see me, he will have to make the best of it, for I mean to stay at peace with him."

She gave a little sigh of relief at his words. "I am so glad." She thought for a moment. "Would you rather go alone?"

"No!" he said. "Come with me for protection, Cressy. I am quite afraid of him, you know." His face was humorous, but she was surprised to hear his voice shake. "I need you. And we'll bring our son."

"They are good friends," Cressy informed him.

"I am glad of it," he replied. They sat in companionable silence, and then he asked: "Shall we live in town or in the country, Cressy?"

"As you wish, my lord."

"But you have lived here. Why did you come here, Cressy, if the country is an indifferent matter to you?"

"In your absence, sir, it seemed the place to be," was all she said.

"Well, I would like to live in the country myself. I have a small estate, not far from here, that I've never stayed at much myself, or managed, but it belongs to me. This past year I've grown quite used to country life, and interested in it. We would keep our Town House still, of course, and go from time to time. You'd shop and I'd—"

"Be gay, my lord?"

"I'm tired of that," he said. "No—" his eyes danced—"I'd shop with you. But you don't need me, Cressy. That's a damned becoming frock."

"I need you very much, my lord."

"Do you? I wonder. Well, tell your father that. But I think that I have done you little good."

She just laughed at him, and looked meaningly at the little boy near their feet, and put her fingers on his lips to stop his vein of talk. "We were not gay at all, while you were gone," she said.

"You were not like Cressid, then? No Diomède? To Troilius, you've been true, all these two years?"

"Like Cressid, sir?" She thought him serious, though she did not understand him.

"A story I read while I was gone. Cressida is your namesake. She was a Greek, and very beautiful, and not entirely faithful."

"You are too foolish, my lord," she said, "to answer, and so I shall not. Do you pick a quarrel with me?" Her smile belied her words.

"I do," he said, "and here's the settlement," and kissed her, and his son.

The next morning he ordered his curricle to be brought round, and took his wife and child out driving. He gave his whip to the little boy, who bit it.

"He'll grow up to be a 'whip,' that one," he remarked. "I think while we are out, we'll let your father know of your return and my arrival, before someone else informs him."

If it was his wish to surprise, and unnerve the Duke, he achieved it. His Grace was walking on his estate, and they walked out, Gore carrying his son, to meet him. He saw them coming, incredulously, with violent, conflicting emotions. He could not mistake the Marquis' figure, and he could not imagine what greeting to expect from a man he had thought to have buried alive, and had since thought buried in earth. If the Marquis' revenge was to expose and castigate him in his daughter's presence, he saw no help for it. As they neared him, he did not move. His face stiffened into a mask, behind which his eyes looked out coldly and warily.

"I have come back, Beau-père," the Marquis said in a light, expressionless voice. There was a silence.

"I see indeed you have, Beau-fils," his Grace answered, his

tone matching the tone of the Marquis, "and I am wondering how. One thought that you were dead."

"Your daughter came to fetch me, when I wrote her, and to bring me funds," the Marquis said simply, avoiding the Duke's remark, and offering him several possibilities to think on.

"You were where, or may one ask?" the Duke's light careful tone continued, offering him a clear opening, but the Marquis chose to answer only what the Duke could not know.

"A farm near Normandy, I forget the name. Labouring."

Surprise came into the Duke's face which increased when the Marquis unexpectedly dropped to one knee before him and took his hand and briefly bowed his head over it in salutation.

"Get up, Gore!" the Duke exclaimed testily. "You are absurd. What does this signify?"

The Marquis raised his head and looked up at him, his lips parted, and smiled slightly, but he did not rise. "A wish for peace," he said. "You have met—my son?"

"Many times," the Duke said, noting inwardly the claim. "Get up, you silly boy!"

The Marquis obediently rose and without comment walked beside the Duke, his eyes studiously cast down. Cressy and the child had wandered a little way from them, and for a time they simply watched the pair in silence.

"We've only met, you know," the Marquis said, continuing their last remarks. He turned his gaze direct upon the Duke. "I thought I'd like to watch my child grow up."

"A natural wish," replied the Duke, "and one that hardly needs to be expressed to me."

"I hoped that you would think so," the Marquis said intently.

"You have changed, Gore, since I saw you last," the Duke remarked curiously, not really changing their subject.

"I think I have, your Grace," the Marquis said quietly.

"You have suffered, too?" It was more a statement than a question.

"I have, my lord."

"It is strange," the Duke said, "but I had not thought I would be pleased with your return. I find I am."

"I am glad," the Marquis said simply. "I wish to be friends with the sire of my dear wife." He looked carefully at a distant tree and picked his words. "As I remember, there was between us at one time a—dispute—on which we could not come to an agreement. I have since thought to tell you that you were in the right, as you well knew, and as I would not admit, and to tell you that I am sorry to have given you cause ever to be vexed with me."

"Why do you say these things to me now?" the Duke asked heavily, and rather sadly.

"I am tired of journeys. My son grows." He took the child's hand, for the baby had come near him. "I hope to know him, and also my next child which I think I have already given my wife."

Cressy blushed and gasped, incoherently, "My lord! Then you did know!"

"Of course I knew," he said, looking straightly at her. "What do you take me for?" She blushed again.

"It would seem you two are at accord," the Duke observed, somewhat dryly.

"It would so seem," the Marquis replied, unabashed.

"Take the boy into the house, Cressy, and find him cakes," her father directed. "We will follow you, more slowly." They stood again in silence, watching the two, the small slender girl and the hopping sturdy child.

"You will think that I have done wrong by you," finally offered the Duke.

"I have not said so," replied the Marquis, regarding him steadily.

"You look well, considering," the Duke said inconsequently. Then he looked directly at the Marquis. "I did not mean it for the best for you, I meant it for the worst."

"I know that," said the Marquis. "But in the end it has not turned out so badly as we either thought for." The Duke made no reply, for none seemed required. "I have written a paper," the Marquis continued quietly, his gaze removed, "in which I have described the author of my recent journey. It is not my wish to speak of that journey, to you or to my father or to anyone," he added carefully. "For my part, it is something best forgotten. It happened. It is done. I carry no grudges about it. But if there should be a repetition of such things, I have made careful provision how the letter should be opened. You understand my meaning?"

"Perfectly," said the Duke. "I join you in your wish that the letter remain unopened. I trust it will." They had reached the house now, and they stood just outside the door.

The Marquis did not offer to go in. He was looking at the Duke with unusual hesitation, and finally he brought himself to speak: "May I ask one question of you now?"

"You may ask," the Duke replied unencouragingly.

"Did Cressy ask you to—do what you did—remove me?" A flush crept slowly up his cheeks.

"What difference would such knowledge make to you?" the Duke answered, still forbiddingly.

"None, I think, but I should like to know."

"She did not know of it."

"I know that, but did she ask you?" The Marquis waited, taut, expectant.

The Duke slightly shook his head. "She did not ask me to. I think you must not know her. She told me very little. I found my reasons for myself." The lines in the Marquis' face eased, and he looked younger suddenly, more his age. The Duke to his surprise was moved. "And I will tell you one thing more. She did not forget you ever, Gore, at any time, though I endeavoured at it, with my best—or worst—intentions. Cressy is as stubborn as you ever were. Look to it."

They went into the Duke's study in comparative amity, and joined Cressy and the Duke's grandson for tea. No one watching them would have imagined there had ever been discord between them. The twins, come in from hunting, did watch them and were amazed. They displayed some embarrassment at first, but in the lack of any on the part of the Marquis and the Duke and their adoring nephew, they forgot their own. The Marquis was well pleased with his visit. The sight of the faces of his several tormentors at his sudden unheralded appearance had afforded him a wicked, and he felt, deserved gratification. Moreover, he was pleased to be friends with Cressy's family for her sake. He felt, though, that he had a last unfinished business.

"He said to her, driving slowly on the way home: "When I

saw you just before I left, those months ago, I asked your pardon. Do you remember?"

"I remember very well."

"Did you understand for what?" She did not answer him or encourage him.

"Cressy, I have something to confess."

"Do not, my lord." She reached her fingers against his lips.

"Cressy, it *was* I."

"My dear, I always knew."

"You knew?" He was amazed.

"You wanted me to think it was not you, and so I did not like to say it was."

He began to laugh, helplessly. "You do make fools of men, you women."

"You make the more of us, my lord."

"*How* did you know, when I made sure you shouldn't? What thing betrayed me?

"How could I not, my lord? Your scent, the shadows on your face, the outline of your brow and nose, your crooked tooth, the length beneath your chin, your neck, the way you bear your chest, your laugh, your voice, the fingers on your hands, a thousand thousand things. I thought at first it must be you, and then I felt I must have been mistaken, but in the end I always knew." She looked at him quickly, and then away. He had kept his eyes fixed on her during her catalogue of his parts, but they had not yet gone off the road. "Why, why else did you think I lay so still, my lord?"

He digested this, and then he asked curiously, "What is my scent?"

"You smell of shrimp at certain times, my lord," she said demurely, and heard his breath draw in. "But there is one thing I have wanted to ask you. Why, dear Bysshe? I never understood."

"It was a bet," he said. "I won."

"A bet, my lord?" Words failed her.

"A vile, foolish, brutal, stupid bet. But how I won!" He bent and kissed her quietly, and then helped her and his son to descend, for by this time they had reached home.

ABOUT THE AUTHOR

Born in Dallas, Lolah Burford now lives in Fort Worth with her husband, William Burford the poet, and their three young daughters. She graduated from Bryn Mawr and is a scholar of eighteenth-century England. *Vice Avenged: A Moral Tale* is her first book.